This book belongs to

_____

Children's
POOLBEG

ROBBERS ON THE STREETS

A Paperback Original
First Published 1990 by
Poolbeg Press Ltd.,
Knocksedan House,
Swords, Co. Dublin, Ireland

ISBN 1 85371 113 6

Cover design by Steven Hope
Typeset by Seton Music Graphics Ltd,
Bantry, Co. Cork
Printed by The Guernsey Press Ltd.,
Vale, Guernsey, Channel Islands

ROBBERS
ON THE
STREETS
Carolyn Swift

POOLBEG

For Ben and all the many others who helped,
but might not wish to be named.

Chapter Rhyme

Hard-up, let down and knocked about,
Have it yourself or be without;
Trust nobody when there's a shadow of doubt
Are you spin, spout or real black out!

Contents

Contents

1
HARD-UP

ay Byrne had hardly closed the door of her house behind her when she heard her name shouted from across the road.

"May! May! Give us a push!"

"Ah, Brendan, you're a little pest!" she protested.

All the same, she crossed the road to the row of brightly coloured swings in the middle of the Square, where her youngest brother sat with a group of small boys around him.

"You're only getting the one push now!" she warned him, drawing the seat of the swing back towards her.

As she released the swing she saw Mr Reilly come out of his house on the opposite side of the Square and hurry off around the

1

corner. May knew where he was going. It was Tuesday, and Tuesday was the day he went to sign on at the Cumberland Street Labour Exchange and draw his unemployment assistance.

People knew things like that about their neighbours when they lived in the Square. It was hard to keep secrets in the rows of little houses that faced each other beneath the shadow of the Four Courts. Everyone knew everyone else, but May knew more than most people about what went on in the Reilly home, because Maura Reilly was almost her best friend.

"Higher!" Brendan squealed in delight. "Higher!"

"This is the last go!" May said, as she drew the swing back even further. As she let it go again something else caught her eye on the far side of the Square. A large woman with brassy hair and a red coat with a fur collar had come round the corner from the direction in which Mr Reilly had gone. She went straight to the Reilly's door and rapped smartly on it.

At once the door shot open as if Mrs Reilly had been standing right behind it. She was already wearing her headscarf. She looked furtively around as if to make sure there was no-one about and then set off at a brisk trot by the side of the large woman. She hadn't noticed May across the Square, half-hidden by the swings and the group of boys.

"Again! Again!" Brendan shouted.

"I told you that was the last go," May said firmly. "I've to go to Mac's for the messages!"

Then, before he could start a scene, May walked briskly between the row of little posts that stopped cars from driving into the Square. As she reached Chancery Street she glanced to her left and saw Mrs Reilly and the large woman in the red coat passing the Bridewell Garda Station. For a moment she stopped and watched them turn into Church Street, before heading off in the opposite direction.

She felt uneasy about seeing Mrs Reilly in the company of that woman because she knew who she was. She was known to everyone in the Square as Ma Mulcahy and she was a money lender.

May thought about Ma Mulcahy as she walked back from Mac's with her full shopping bag. Ma Mulcahy did not live in the Square but over in the Flats. All the same, she was no stranger in the Square these days.

Of course, lots of people called to the Square who did not actually live there. There was Mrs Cullen, who lived over in Stirrup Lane, but then she was Mrs Doyle's sister. There were people collecting for the pools and for the Christmas Club. There were people selling things door to door like Cut-Price Joe and the Box of Tricks Man. There were uncles and aunts, nieces and nephews, friends and acquaintances, but Ma Mulcahy was nobody's friend. If she called to the Square it was on business and business that boded no good for anyone but Ma Mulcahy.

May remembered then what her father had said one Sunday when her mother had mentioned Ma Mulcahy.

"Whatever you do," he had ordered, "stay out of the clutches of that loan shark. Wouldn't you think people would have more sense than to go running to her?"

"There's some poor souls have no choice," her mother had argued. "These are bad times."

"Things are never so bad they can't be worse," her father had said then. "Mark my words, Mary! I never knew the one that went to Ma Mulcahy that didn't end up the worst for it."

May knew that things were bad at the Reilly's. They had been bad ever since Mr Reilly had lost his job as a porter when they had moved the Dublin Fruit and Vegetable Market. Mrs Reilly worked at the contract cleaning but that never seemed to bring in enough money for their needs and Mr Reilly's needs seemed to have grown since he lost his job and had so much more drinking time. Things had got better for a while last year, when Maura was getting paid every week for singing on the telly, but that had only lasted a couple of months. Then the series was over and Maura had had to go back to school in September. Now Ma Mulcahy was calling to their door.

As she came to St. Mary's Abbey, May saw old Danny Noonan ahead of her. The old sailor was hobbling along, stiff from his arthritis and weighed down with the library books he was carrying.

May quickly overtook him and then slowed down to keep pace beside him, for the old man had been a trusted friend to all the young people in the Square ever since he had become too old and lame to go to sea any longer.

"Danny," she said, because it was the thing that was uppermost in her mind, "Did you ever go to Ma Mulcahy?"

"Now why would I do a foolish thing like that?" Danny asked. "Haven't I my bit of a pension and the best friends and neighbours anyone could want if I'd be short of the bit of tea or sugar till the Friday? And haven't I the free bus and the free fuel and the free black and white telly? And the free gas and the books from the Public Library round the corner in Capel Street? And your mother, God bless her, to do the bit of washing for me and the odd bit of cleaning. There's not a lot an old man needs when he's already seen the world. If the Eastern Health Board would only give me a new pair of legs now, the way I could keep warm by running around in the winter and not be using up the fuel so fast, I wouldn't swap places with the Taoiseach's granny!"

"My da says that no-one should ever go to Ma Mulcahy," May persisted.

"And he never said a truer word," old Danny agreed. "For once Ma Mulcahy has you in her clutches she'll squeeze you dry."

"She called to Mrs Reilly this morning," May told him.

"She did," Danny nodded. "Wasn't I coming out of the newsagent's in Church Street, after getting a bit of tobacco for the old pipe, when I saw Mrs Reilly going into the post office for the children's allowance."

"And was Ma Mulcahy with her?" May asked.

"Waiting outside," Danny said. "It was her I saw first, letting on to be looking in the newsagent's window."

"Why was she waiting outside?" May asked, puzzled.

"To get the children's allowance off of Mrs Reilly, of course," Danny explained. "That way she's sure of getting the weekly repayments on the loan she gave Mrs Reilly to get the few extras for the Christmas."

"That's mean," May said. "If I was Mrs Reilly, I'd collect the allowance before Ma Mulcahy called."

"You would not," Danny told her, "for Ma Mulcahy holds the allowance book. She calls for Mrs Reilly, goes to the post office with her, gives her the book at the door and then waits outside to take book and money off of her when she comes out again. She's been at that a good while now on the first Tuesday, only you weren't here to see her on account of being at school."

"How d'you know she takes the money, Danny?" May demanded. "Did you see her take it?"

"There was no need," Danny said. "That's the way Ma Mulcahy works. If ever you see her of a first Tuesday near the post office, that's what she's at."

"But how's Mrs Reilly to manage without the allowance?" May asked. "Maura's not earning now and she says her Da never brings home much out of his labour money. Mrs Reilly's never going to manage the rent and the food and everything out of what she gets for the contract cleaning!"

"And she'll be lucky if she gets to keep all of that," Danny told her. "The way Ma Mulcahy works out the weekly payments, the allowance for one child is little enough."

"Oh, poor Mrs Reilly," May cried. "No wonder she looks so miserable. I wish there was something I could do to help."

"And you may go on wishing," Danny said, "barring you win the lottery. Mrs Reilly should have had the sense not to get mixed up with that one in the first place."

"Don't you know well that Mr Reilly was expecting his Christmas dinner and a few bottles of something to go with it?" May pointed out. "And she gave Maura an anorak for her Christmas box, as well as putting something down on a new winter coat for herself. You could near see through her old one, it had gone that thin. The week of the frost she was only blue with the cold and the price of fuel the way it is."

Danny nodded. He knew well enough how things were with the Reillys.

"I want you to promise me something, May," he said. "Will you do that for me, like a good girl?"

"What is it, Danny?"

"The day you draw your first pay packet, go down to the Credit Union over in Beresford Street and give them a pound. That way you'll never be in the trouble Mrs Reilly's in this minute. Once you join the Credit Union, they'll look after you, even if you were never to earn another penny, but you'd be the wise girl to give them the few bob whenever you have it, for the more you give them, the more they can lend you when you're suddenly strapped for it. Do you promise me now?"

"I do, Danny," May said solemnly, "and no matter what, I'll never go next or near Ma Mulcahy."

"There's many a one said that till his back was to the wall," Danny told her, "but the way to make sure you stick to your word is to join the Credit Union."

* * *

A fine rain was falling as Richie, Whacker and Mickser left the ball alley beside Green Street Courthouse and hurried down Halston Street. At the back of the market site, the road had been dug up again and Richie slipped on the wet cobblestones and nearly stumbled into the hole.

"Mind the pothole," Whacker shouted, grabbing Richie by the arm.

"Yeah, mind it real well!" one of the lads behind them giggled. "That pothole's me Mammy's pride and joy!"

"Listen to the funny man!" said Richie, as the whole group became convulsed with laughter, but he did not say it too loudly. The boys behind them were older and bigger than they were and there was no point in sticking his neck out. They were a pretty tough bunch out of the flats and Richie was not sorry when they swung right towards Greek Street and left Whacker, Mickser and himself to push on towards the Square by themselves.

"What did he mean about the pothole, Redser?" Whacker asked, as they found themselves on their own again.

"Nothing," Richie told him. "Jemmo Mulcahy goes in for the repartee, that's all!"

"Not if what I hear is true," Mickser said. "I heard that he goes in for the fast plate switching too."

"The what?" Richie ran a hand through his curly red hair, already damp from the drizzle.

"Same as for the three-card trick," Mickser told him. "It's the quickness of the hand deceives the eye. Your man Jemmo doesn't pinch the cars himself, of course. Nothing so chancey! But when the fellow that did the job drives into the shed up the lane, there's Jemmo and the brother, waiting for him with the false plates all ready. One, two, three and they have the old plates off, the new ones on, a quick spray and the job is oxo. And all within an ass's bawl of the Bridewell. No wonder Jemmo Mulcahy fancies himself."

Whacker gave a whistle. "Where did you hear that one, Mickser?"

"Oh, I keep my ears open. Jemmo likes to impress the gang up at the ball alley. I'd say he makes a good few bob out of the plate-switching game."

"He wouldn't do it otherwise," Whacker agreed. "Those Mulcahys will do anything for money and nothing whatsoever without it!"

They had reached the point just beyond the posts where they had to go in different directions: Richie straight on to the Byrnes' house opposite the swings, Whacker left to the Kellys' and Mickser across the Square to the Dolans'. Usually they would stop about here, chatting of this and that. Today it was too wet.

"See you tomorrow!" they called to each other, as they each ran off to their own doors.

As Whacker opened his, the sound of police sirens, shouts and gunfire came from the telly. He went into the room and plonked himself down on the couch in front of the set beside his sister Imelda, who gave a little scream.

"You're as bad as that Chrissie on the box," Mr Kelly told her. "Isn't her screaming bad enough without you at it as well!"

"But this fella's only soaking!" Imelda protested. "I don't want him dripping all over me."

"Go on outa that!" Whacker retorted. "The jacket's a bit damp, that's all. Can you never add two and two without making forty out of it?"

"Patrick Kelly," his mother ordered, "will you get those wet things off of you and out of here this instant! Have you no sense at all?"

Whacker groaned, but did as he was told. He knew when his mother called him Patrick it was not the moment to argue. But when he came back the end credits were rolling over the shot of the two detectives.

"Now you've made me miss it!" he complained.

"It was near over anyway," his mother said. "I'm going to put the kettle on."

"What's on the other side?" Whacker asked, as the RTE logo came up on the screen, but his father's head was already buried in the sports page of the evening paper.

"Will you give us a look at the paper for a second, Da?" Imelda asked. "We want to see what's on the other side."

"Leave it where it is", Mr. Kelly said. "The World Cup's on after the news."

"Oh no!" moaned Imelda. "Not again!"

"You don't have to watch it if you don't want to," Whacker retorted. The newscaster had begun to read the headlines, but Whacker was not really listening. He was hunting for his chart of World Cup fixtures and results to date.

"Malicious injuries claims against Dublin Corporation have doubled," the voice of the newscaster continued. "Later in the programme Finance Officer Ignatius Hill explains the Corporation's insurance problems."

Whacker had found his chart under a pile of women's magazines. His mother had been tidying again. He shut his ears to the sound of the newscaster's voice and concentrated on his chart.

*   *   *

Maura heard her father stumble in the hall on his way to the kitchen. That was a sure sign that there would not be too much of the labour money left. She hoped he wasn't in bad humour. She dreaded Friday evenings when her father was late in and her mother had already left for work.

The kettle was nearly boiled dry, though she had put a fresh one on the cooker with the heat turned down low soon after her mother went out. She hoped there would be enough in it for the tea. Her father hated having to wait while she boiled up fresh water.

He was in the kitchen now, looking at the table, bare of everything but the sliced pan, tub of margarine and ketchup bottle.

"Where's me dinner?" he asked sharply. "I'm famished for the want of it."

"Mammy left spuds sliced ready for the chips", Maura told him, wetting the tea.

Luckily there was just enough water left in the kettle to fill the pot. "There was no sense cooking them till you came. Chips go soggy on you if you try to keep them hot. They won't be long."

"Is that all I'm getting?"

Maura gave him a nervous glance, as she turned up the heat under the chip pan. He was feeling the front of the oven. It was cold, of course. What had he expected, she wondered: a thick juicy steak keeping hot inside?

"I'm frying you an egg," she told him, "and there's a few beans left from yesterday in the small pan."

"It's well for your mother she's not here to face me," her father grumbled, "putting the likes of that on the table for a grown man at the end of a day's fasting. But I should know better by now than look for to be treated like the head of the house. She'll be telling me that she's the breadwinner now, though it's little enough she brings back at the end of the day. I suppose she ate her fill before she left."

"She did not then," Maura cried indignantly, stung into defending her mother though she knew it was only foolish to answer him back. "She'd nothing only bread and marg."

"Well, if she's at that slimming lark she needn't be dragging me into it!" He drew back his chair from the table and slumped into it. "Women go in for that class of foolishness but a working man needs his grub."

Maura checked herself from asking him what work he had been doing that day. It was not his fault, she thought, that he had lost his job at a time when all the bosses were looking for younger men. She set the teapot down on the table at her father's elbow. Then she lifted the chips in their wire mesh basket and gave them a bit of a shake. They were a nice golden brown. Another few minutes and they would be ready. She turned up the heat under the beans, cracked the egg on the side of the sink and broke it carefully into the frying pan.

"I'll see if I can get some sort of a job for the holidays," she said, as she tipped the chips on to the plate she had left warming on the sink. "If I can't get a singing job I can always go cleaning with Mammy."

"Of course, the likes of you can walk in and out of jobs at will," her father said. "It's only men with a lifetime's experience behind them that nobody wants."

"It's not easy for anyone to get work these times," Maura said, spooning the beans on to the plate beside the chips. "But the contract cleaners sometimes look for people to fill in if somebody would be out sick. And if you're tall enough they don't ask about your age when they're stuck for a few days."

She slid the egg carefully from the pan on to the plate and put it in front of her father.

"Them chips is greasy," he said in disgust, lifting one with his fork and letting it fall to the plate again. "Do you not know enough to drain them on a piece of newspaper?"

"I didn't have any newspaper," Maura told him and then added in spite of herself, "and if you don't want the chips I'll have them. I had nothing only bread and marg. for tea. We saved the egg and beans for you."

"I don't know what your mother does with the money," her father said irritably, eating the chips despite the grease.

"What money?" Maura snapped.

"Hasn't she all her earnings, your allowance and the labour money every week?"

He drew three tenners from his pocket and slapped them down on the table as if they were hundreds.

"Things are gone very dear," Maura told him. "You'd find out quick enough if you had to be buying the food."

"Don't be giving me cheek!" her father snarled. "There's Mrs Doyle now, putting rashers and sausages on the table every day and look at the football team she has in the house!"

He took a slice of bread and wiped it around his plate to mop up the despised grease. Then he drained his cup.

"It's poor welcome I get in this house now," he said, "so I'll go where I'll be among friends!"

He pushed back his chair, rose with dignity and staggered as he reached for his jacket. Maura knew he was off to Flynn's. Hastily she put a plate down on top of the tenners for fear he would notice them and slip them back into his pocket. She might never have got them at all if he had not been showing off his generosity. When she heard the door slam shut behind him she put them carefully into the pocket of her jeans. Then she carried the dirty delf from the table to the sink and began to wash up.

Her father was still in Flynn's when her mother got back from work.

"Merciful hour!" Mrs Reilly cried. "Has he gone off to Flynn's to drink the last of the labour money?"

"I got these off of him," Maura said, giving her mother the tenners.

Her mother looked at them for a moment and then burst into tears.

"What's to become of us?" she sobbed. "What's to become of us?"

Maura put her arm around her mother's shoulders. It was like putting an arm around a skeleton, she thought, realizing for the first time how thin and bony her mother had grown.

"We'll manage somehow," she said. "On Monday I'll start looking for a job for the holidays."

"What's the use?" Tears trickled down her mother's cheeks. "There'll never be enough to pay off Ma Mulcahy. And she says to have the rest of the sixteen pound by next Friday or she'll tell your father."

"Then let her!" shouted Maura angrily. "Wasn't he complaining about not getting rashers and sausages? Rashers and sausages, if you don't mind, and he stuffing himself with the egg, beans and chips the two of us went without! And then he wanted to know what you did with the money! It's good enough for him if Ma Mulcahy gets on to him instead of you for a change!"

"Are you mad?" her mother cried. "He'll only murder me!"

"But he must know," Maura argued. "I think he only lets on not to. Didn't he find out long ago, the time he...?"

She broke off in mid-sentence. Her mother never talked about that day, even though she must know that Maura had heard her father shouting and the sound of the door slamming behind him. When she had noticed Maura looking at the little trickle of blood at the corner of her mouth, she had grabbed a tissue and let on to have a nose bleed, but now her mother seemed to have done with pretending.

"He thinks the loan was paid off!" she sobbed.

"How could he?" Maura cried. "Where does he think the money came from? I know you paid off some of it when I got the money for the telly, but Da needed new shoes. Then you got sick and couldn't do the cleaning for a week. That's when Ma Mulcahy took the allowance book. Why would he think the loan was paid off?"

"Because I told him so, that's the why! I know I shouldn't be telling him lies, but he had me scared. You know how he is when he's jarred..."

Maura nodded. The time her father had found out about Ma Mulcahy was not the only time her mother had had nose bleeds.

"Maybe if we both talked to him," she suggested uncertainly. "Explained how hard it is to manage, like…"

Her mother only shook her head.

"I have to find money some way," she said. "If Ma Mulcahy goes to your father and he finds out I lied to him, this time he'll really murder me!"

2
LET DOWN AND KNOCKED ABOUT

ext morning, Maura called over to the Byrnes', looking for May, for that was what she had always done when she was worried about anything.

Patchie ran, barking, to greet her, jumping all over her and covering her hands and bare arms with affectionate licks. Any friend of May was a friend of Patchie, though May had been only a toddler when Mr Byrne had got him from the dog's home as a pup for a Christmas box for Richie

"Down, Patchie, down!" Maura cried, but she gave him a little hug all the same. She wished that they had a dog at home, though she supposed it would only be one more mouth to feed just now. All the same, it seemed unfair that May, with three brothers at home, should also have a dog when she, who had neither brother nor sister, had none. It would be less lonely waiting for her father to come home on a Tuesday evening if they had a dog.

"We're just tidying up after the breakfast," May said. "Come on in."

Richie was putting the last of the plates into the rack to drain as they arrived and Maura wished again that she had a brother to help with the chores, but she supposed if she had he would be like her father. He never so much as rinsed a glass. Mrs Byrne had always made Richie take his turn at sweeping the floor or washing up, so that now he did it without even thinking about it. Once, long ago, Mickser's older brother had teased him about it, but Richie had fought the bigger boy until he was forced to admit that there was nothing cissie about Richie.

"I was thinking of going out to RTE to ask was there any work going," Maura began, not wanting to talk about her mother in front of Richie.

"Oh," May cried, "wouldn't it be great if there was?"

"Would you ever come with me?" Maura asked. "I'd feel foolish going on my own."

"We'll all go!" Richie cried. "They might have work for us all again, like they did last year."

"And wouldn't we look right eejits, all traipsing out there on spec?" May argued. "Maura's the only one they'd want for anything only extra work and she can tell them if there's anything going in that line we're free and would like to do it."

"They might have something for Whacker," Richie told her, "and Theo likes him."

"They're hardly looking for break dancers every day of the week," May said flatly, "and he can't try for trainee technician till he leaves school. We'll only spoil Maura's chances if we all go."

"Six people turning up without being asked might look a bit funny," Maura agreed apologetically, "but I'll make sure they know we're all free for the holidays. Let's go this morning, May. Then if they've nothing for me I could see tonight if there's anything going at the contract cleaners."

As they turned their bikes out of the traffic at the side of Donnybrook Church nearly an hour later, Maura finished telling May all that had happened at home.

"But I hate the old contract cleaning," she added, "and they pay awful little."

"If RTE paid you as much as they did last year," May asked, "would it see you right?"

Maura shook her head.

"But it would pay the sixteen pound every week for the while I'd be working," she said, "so Mammy could get back the allowance book and her coat off of Mr Leventon."

"She never pawned her good new coat?" May asked, shocked.

"She ran down to Capel Street with it first thing this morning," Maura told her. "She says she won't be needing it again till the weather turns cold, but she only got a few pound on it. I wouldn't mind but she was ages paying for it on the never never."

"If I get any extra work, I'll give you the lend of a loan," May said, but Maura shook her head again.

I wouldn't take it off you, May," she said. "We owe that much as it is. We'd want to win the lottery to get ourselves straight again. If I land something with RTE I'm going to get a ticket every week from this out."

"It's terrible chancey," May said.

She had heard her father often enough on the subject of the National Lottery. He was always giving out about money going out every week and nothing ever coming back.

But a ticket was only a pound. It was two pounds in to the bingo and her mother and Mrs Kelly went there together every Wednesday night. And you could win an awful lot more on the lottery than you could at the bingo.

"Maybe it would be worth a try," she agreed, as they put their bikes into the stands under the colonnade of the studio building and went in through the main door into reception.

"I want to see Mr Theo Sylvester," Maura said to the girl on the desk.

"Have you an appointment?"

"Tell him Maura Reilly and May Byrne want to see him," May cut in, as Maura fell back, defeated.

"Very well. Take a seat over there, please", the receptionist said, waving them over to some chairs along the wall.

"I suppose we should have phoned," Maura said glumly, as they sank into the low chairs.

"Theo wouldn't refuse to see us," May said. "Not after the note Sylvia sent me."

"I dunno," Maura said. "Suppose he's busy?"

The receptionist, who had been speaking into her telephone, waved at them to come back to the desk.

"I'm afraid he's not here today," she said. "He's at a meeting in London."

"Well, is Michael Casey here?" May said quickly, before the receptionist could go back to her book.

The receptionist picked up a dictionary, thumbed through it and dialled a number.

"There are two young girls down here asking to see Mr Casey," she said. "Maura Reilly and May Byrne... I see. All right, I'll tell them."

"Mr Casey's not here either," she said, "but his PA's coming down to you."

"Bea!" Maura cried. "That will be every bit as good as seeing Michael."

But the girl who came down the stairs and over to them with a look of enquiry on her face was not Bea. She was broad-shouldered with long dark hair, as different as she could possibly be from the slim, fair-haired girl they had worked with the year before.

"You were looking for Michael Casey?" she said. "I'm afraid he's on leave. I'm his PA. Can I help you?"

"Isn't Bea Carr his PA any more then?" May asked, as Maura stood tongue-tied.

"Bea's working as a vision-mixer now," the girl said. "Is that who you want to see?"

"Oh no," Maura cried. "It's just that she worked on the series I was on last year."

"Of course!" the girl said, sounding more friendly now. "I knew the name rang a bell! Can I give Michael a message for you when he comes back on Monday week?"

"I was hoping he might have work for me, maybe," Maura blurted out.

"I see," the girl said, sounding less friendly again. "Well, I'll tell him you called as soon as I see him. Do we have a telephone number for you?"

"We don't have a phone," Maura began, haltingly, but May cut in.

"You can contact us by ringing Flynns. That's what Bea did all last summer. The number must be on the files. And would you tell him all six of us are free if there's anything going?"

"Will he know what that means?" the girl asked, looking down her nose at them.

"Of course he will," May said. "We're friends of his!" and she turned on her heel and marched angrily out of the door.

Maura hesitated, embarrassed, then ran out after her.

"Oh, May, you shouldn't have snapped at her like that! Now she won't even give him the message."

"Oh yes, she will," May said. "That's why I did it. Because we're still at school she mightn't have bothered her head. Now she'll be scared not to!"

But even she felt depressed as they rode back down the driveway towards the side gate. With Michael away for ten days, he would never be able to find Maura a job in time to get the Reillys out of trouble. There was nothing for it now but the contract cleaning.

* * *

Meanwhile, Whacker and Richie were on their way back from North Brunswick Street. Mr Kelly was doing a plumbing job in a house over by the school and Mrs Kelly had sent Whacker across with a message. When she had cornered him, he was in the middle of an argument with Richie over whether the referee had been blind or blind drunk to give a free against Ireland and, to avoid interrupting the argument, they had gone to North Brunswick Street together. Turning into Chancery Street on their way home, they saw people surging out of the gates leading to the District Court. Shouting and laughing, they poured on to the street, spilling over the curb on to the roadway.

"Someone must have got probation!" grinned Whacker. "They look real pleased with themselves!"

"There's Jemmo and the brother with Ma Mulcahy," Richie said. "And Con Twomey's there too."

"That little twister!" Whacker muttered. "Any DJ that gave him probation must have been dozing. He'd sell his grandmother to zap a few space invaders on the gaming machines!"

"Looks like someone zapped him this time," Richie commented. "He's wearing one of those collar things around his neck."

The crowd flowed on ahead of them across Greek Street, still singing and cheering, and Con Twomey was among the noisiest.

"The most of them's out of the flats," Richie went on. "That's the gang were up at the ball alley yesterday."

"Whatever had that shower in the District Court?" Whacker wondered aloud. "They look like they pulled some stroke and now they're off to celebrate."

Richie watched them jostle their way past the Eastern Health Board offices and into the corner pub.

"Well," he said, "we'll hear soon enough, you can be sure of that. Anything that would have that crowd knocking back pints and small ones this early in the week won't stay secret for long!"

But it was several days later before they heard anything more about it and even that was only due to Mickser.

"There was Con Twomey," he told Whacker, "swanking passed the ball alley in a new black leather jacket—Con Twomey, that never had any decent gear in his life! I asked him where he got it and he winked at Jemmo Mulcahy and said he just fell in for it. Then Jemmo and the rest of them near burst themselves laughing like he'd said something real smart!"

"The way they did the time I near fell into the pothole," Richie agreed.

Suddenly Whacker made a sort of choking sound.

"Did you say 'fell,' Redser?" he gasped.

Richie and Mickser turned to look at him. His mouth hung open and his jaw worked as if he were chewing invisible gum. It was the way he always looked before he surprised everyone in class by coming out with the answer to the six marker that no-one else had been able to get and Richie knew by now that it meant that Whacker was thinking.

"Of course," Richie told him. "D'you not remember? You said to mind the hole and Jemmo said to mind it real well."

"That's right," Whacker nodded, "and it puts me in mind of something I heard on the telly the other day. Tell me this, Mickser, and tell me no more: was Con Twomey wearing one of them collar-things around his neck?"

Mickser looked at him as if he had two heads.

"Why would he be wearing a collar?" he asked. "Wasn't he in a tee-shirt, same as usual?"

"Whacker means one of them white surgical collars, like they used give out in Jervis Street when people hurt their necks in a car smash," Richie explained. "Had Con Twomey one of them?"

Mickser shook his head.

"Then maybe he fell into the very same hole as Richie," Whacker suggested, "only he did it by accident on purpose like!"

"But why," Mickser asked, "would anyone fall into a pothole on purpose?"

"To claim compensation off of the Corpo, of course," Whacker said. "So long as you could get a doctor to certify you'd done yourself an injury and witnesses to tell how you'd fallen into the pothole they were careless enough to leave lying around!"

"And you wouldn't have to look too far for witnesses if you said you'd give them a few bob out of the compensation," Richie agreed.

"Specially if their names were Jemmo and Patser Mulcahy!" Whacker pointed out.

"Or even Ma Mulcahy herself!" Richie added. "Remember Jemmo saying the pothole was his Mammy's pride and joy?"

Whacker gasped again. His brain was working overtime now.

"Remember," he said after a minute or two of furious chewing, "when Mrs. Commiskey over in the flats got the compensation for her sprained ankle?"

"I do, of course," Mickser said. "Didn't she take the whole family to the Isle of Man for a week and buy a video and a fur coat?"

"Well," Whacker continued, "I remember the Da saying then that it was Ma Mulcahy that went with her to the court to swear she'd fallen over the pavement where it was dug up and no lamp lighting. Maybe being a loan shark's only the day job and Ma Mulcahy does compensation claims as a nixer!"

Mickser whistled.

"Nice work if you can get it," he said, "but what's that got to do with Con Twomey not wearing a surgical collar?"

"Because he was wearing one when Richie and I saw him outside the District Court on Wednesday, looking like a man that had just come in for a few bob!" Whacker explained. "But he mustn't have broken his neck altogether if he's the collar off him already!"

Richie laughed.

"No wonder they didn't mind blowing the readies on a few jars," he said.

But when he told the whole story to May, she didn't find it at all funny.

"Pity Mrs Reilly couldn't fall into a pothole," she said bitterly. "There's Maura out nights dusting office desks and her mother still has to run to the pawn."

"She can't have much left to pawn by now," Richie said, "barring she's leaving down the furniture."

"I wouldn't say she had," May agreed.

"She'd better have a word with Ma Mulcahy so!" Richie said. "I don't see why she shouldn't organise a little compensation for Mrs Reilly while she's about it. God knows, she's making enough out of her!"

But Ma Mulcahy was the last person in the world that Mrs Reilly would have thought of turning to for help. The loan shark's threat to tell Mr. Reilly about the money that was owing had driven her back to Leventon's again and again.

Next day, Maura was tidying her room when she heard her father's voice rising in anger from the kitchen below. It was a sound she had come to dread and she froze beside the open window while his words carried up to her as clearly as if she had been in the kitchen herself.

"D'you think I'm an eejit altogether?" he demanded, "for a man would want to be blind not to see what you're at, going out every night and not back till all hours!"

"For pity's sake," her mother shouted, "amn't I out polishing floors to put food on the table for the three of us?"

"So you say," her father retorted, "but anyone with two eyes in his head would know you were seeing another man!"

"No, Jack, no!" her mother cried. "That's not true and well you know it. How can you say such a thing?"

"Because I seen you every evening, dolling yourself up!"

"Dolling myself up!" her mother echoed indignantly. "In what, I'd like to know, and I without a stitch to my name!"

"And I suppose you're not letting on to be

single when you're off on your own every night?"

"As God is my judge I amn't! Where in the name of all that's holy did you get such a notion?"

"Then where's the ring I gave you—the ring you swore you'd never leave off your finger while there was breath in your body?"

"I... I lost it."

Even from upstairs, Maura could hear the uncertainty in her mother's voice and knew she was covering up. She guessed the ring had followed the good coat.

"Lost it, did you?" Her father's voice was bitter with sarcasm. "And I suppose you thought because I'd lost my job you might as well lose the ring?"

"No, Jack, no!" her mother cried, and there was fear in her voice now.

"I must have put it down out of my hand somewhere. I've looked and looked for it, but I can't seem to find it..." Her voice trailed off.

"You're lying!" Her father's voice was threatening now. "D'you think you can fool me with a pack of lies the like of that?"

She heard her mother scream and then the door slammed shut. Now there was silence, except for the soft, muffled sound of her mother's sobs.

3
HAVE IT YOURSELF

bout eight o'clock that evening, Richie and Whacker were on their way home from the pictures. They always went to the last of the cheap screenings even though it meant hurrying over their tea. They were passing the old church in Mary Street when they heard the sound of tyres screaming behind them and, turning, saw a blue Ford Granada take the corner of Jervis Street on two wheels. As it roared past them Richie glimpsed a young lad at the wheel and another even younger in the passenger seat beside him.

"88D 173," Whacker read out from the number plate. "That's an almost new car! I'll bet you a dollar the driver's not the registered owner. I bet he..."

But before he could say another word there was a squeal of brakes and the sound of a sickening thud.

"He's hit something!" Richie cried, as the car wavered for a second and then shot across Capel Street and on into Little Mary Street.

"You mean someone!" Whacker shouted. And the two boys ran towards the dark shape lying by the curb ahead of them.

As they got closer they could see it was a boy not much older than themselves and, from the volley of abuse he hurled after the now vanished car, he was obviously still very much alive.

"Are you OK?" Richie asked, bending over him as he struggled to sit up.

Immediately he cried out in pain, clutching his side and Richie noticed a dark stain spreading across his shirt.

"You'd better lie still," he told him. "We'll get help."

"You stay with him, Redser," Whacker said, "and I'll run down to the pub and phone the ambulance."

As Whacker ran off Richie heard women's voices behind him, rising in concern. The boy on the ground heard them too.

"Don't let them touch my stock!" he gasped.

It was then Richie noticed for the first time the cardboard box lying in the gutter where it had been knocked from the boy's hands. The lid had fallen off it and green and white caps were spilling out of it on to the road. Quickly Richie thrust them back into the box, put on the lid and tucked the box under his arm. Looking up, he found a small crowd had appeared out of nowhere.

"What happened?" a man was asking.

"He was hit by a car," Richie told him.

"Ah, the poor boy!" a woman exclaimed. "Is he badly hurted?"

"Look at the blood!" cried another.

"Will yous keep back and let the poor boy breathe!" ordered the man.

"Wait till I put this under his poor head!" a woman said, pushing to Richie's side.

"I have your things safe!" Richie whispered into the boy's ear as he raised his head a little so the woman could shove a folded jacket under it. "Where will I leave them for you?"

"Loftus Lane," the boy muttered. "Give them to Ned Sullivan. You can ask anyone."

Whacker had just got back when Richie heard the clang of the ambulance bell. Thrusting their way through the crowd, the ambulance men lifted the boy carefully on to a stretcher but, before they could load it into the ambulance, Whacker tapped Richie on the shoulder.

"The fuzz!" he whispered and the two boys disappeared around the corner into Jervis Lane.

"Let's get outa here!" Whacker said. "We don't want to get dragged in as witnesses. There's nothing we can tell them anyways. It was just a hit-and-run and the kid himself can tell them that."

"We could tell them the number of the car," Richie argued. "The driver deserves to be nicked for not even stopping to see was he alive or dead!"

"We'd only be wasting our breath," Whacker told him. "That car was probably heading straight for the lane. There'll be a different plate up already or I'm a Corkman. That's why the driver couldn't chance stopping. Let's head for home."

"I've to do a message first," Richie said. "This has to be left over to Loftus Lane. It belongs to your man."

Whacker eyed the box under Richie's arm.

"D'you know what you have there, Redser?" he asked. "We don't want to find ourselves charged with illegal possession or anything."

"Take it easy," Richie told him. "They're only World Cup caps and scarves. Your man must have been selling on the bridge."

They heard the ambulance speed off into the distance, bell clanging, as they set off up Jervis Lane, crossed the junction with Parnell Street and cut into Loftus Lane. A small, wiry man was unloading a van a little way up the lane and Richie asked him where he would find Ned Sullivan.

"That's me," the man said.

"I was asked to give you this," Richie explained, handing him the cardboard box.

The man opened it and counted the caps.

"He only sold two dozen," he said. "Why didn't Tony bring them back himself?"

Richie told him what had happened.

"And I suppose," Ned Sullivan said accusingly, "that you're looking to take over the job?"

Richie opened his mouth to deny it, but Whacker got in ahead of him.

"Well," he said, "you'll need someone, won't you? Tony's going to be out of action for a while, by the looks of him."

Ned Sullivan gave him a searching look.

Then he transferred his gaze to Richie. Finally he seemed satisfied.

"Come back tomorrow around half-nine," he said. "I might have something for you then."

When Richie got home, Maura was just leaving. Instead of stopping as usual to ask was the film any good, she hurried passed him, letting on not to have noticed him. Richie guessed she had probably been crying.

"What's up with your woman?" he asked May.

"She's been laid off from the contract cleaning," May told him. "When she arrived up this evening she was sent home. They told her they were up to full strength again and didn't need her, but Maura thinks someone said something to the supervisor about her age. And her father gave her mother a battering for not wearing her wedding ring."

"What's she supposed to do? Richie asked, "run over to Leventon's every time Mr Reilly drags himself out of Flynn's and ask for the lend of a loan of it?"

"She's scared to tell him it's in the pawn," May said. "Maura was hoping to make enough at the cleaning to get it out, but now that's up the Swanee."

"D'you think would she be any good at the selling?" Richie asked suddenly.

"You mean, in Moore Street?" May shook her head. "Them dealers never take on anyone. They've enough in their own families."

"I wasn't thinking of Moore Street," Richie told her. "I was thinking of flogging things on the bridge and outside the bank and in Henry Street."

May looked at him, wide-eyed.

"Can you see Maura playing hide-and-go-seek with the fuzz?" she asked. "They'd have her up in the District Court first go off! Besides, you need to know someone in the business to get the stuff to flog."

"I got myself a contact tonight," Richie said. "Whacker and I have to see him in the morning. You can make good money at the street selling if the rain keeps off long enough."

"Are you out of your mind?" May asked him. "Da will murder you if he finds out. You know what he's like about breaking the law."

"It's not like knocking things off," Richie argued. "The fuzz never bother the lads flogging jewellery from the stands on the bridge."

"Them fellas have a licence to sell," May said. "When they built the shopping centre where the Dandelion Market was they gave the stallholders stands around the city. The fuzz don't run you when you've a licence."

"And what's a licence only an old piece of paper?" Richie sounded impatient at having obstacles put in his way. "It's all street selling, isn't it? When you've no stand you have to keep your eyes peeled for the fuzz, that's all."

"It's chancy," May said.

"D'you want to help Maura or don't you?"

"I do, of course," May snapped.

"Well then," Richie said, "me and Whacker can get the stuff and we can all do a bit of selling.With six of us at it we'd get Mrs. Reilly's wedding ring back in no time."

"Mammy'd go spare if she thought we were at that lark!" May cried. "Besides, Maura would never go for it."

But if May had only known it, at that very moment Maura was toying with the idea of something a great deal more dangerous.

She had set out for her own home across the Square but, as she got closer to the house, her steps got slower and slower. Her mother would not be back from work for at least an hour. Her father would be there all right. It was a Monday and even with the little he had given her mother, he was out of funds by now. Without the readies to go over to Flynn's he had been in bad humour all day. If she arrived back ahead of her mother he would want to know why.

She dreaded the thought of having to tell him she would be bringing home no more money from the contract cleaning. When she did face him it would be better to have her mother there. She had gone straight to May with the news that she had been laid off. Now she realized she had only put off the evil hour. She would have stayed at the Byrnes' longer, but the sight of Richie had been enough to drive her away. Even though he was almost like a brother to her, she could only talk about her troubles when May was by herself.

Reaching her own front door, she suddenly quickened her step and walked straight on, turning left into East Aran Street and right towards the quays. Only when she was away from the Square did her steps slow again, for she was going nowhere, only filling in the time until her mother got back.

When she reached the quays, she started walking towards the city centre. Just before Capel Street Bridge, she crossed the road and looked over the wall into the river. It was a fine evening and the water sparkled brightly as it flowed under the bridge on its way to the sea. It was less smelly than usual, she thought, but then there had been that spell of rain early in June and the water level was higher than it had been for the past three or four summers.

She wondered what it would be like to jump in off the bridge. The quays were almost deserted, with only the occasional passing car. She had not even had to wait to cross the road. Probably no-one would see her jump, so there would be no-one to raise the alarm or fish her out. Maybe that was why people usually jumped from O'Connell Bridge, where there were always plenty of passers-by. But then, why jump in the first place if you wanted to be fished out?

The idea seemed positively tempting. It would certainly be one way to get out of having to face her father. And then she wouldn't have to worry about paying back Ma Mulcahy or getting her mother's things back out of pawn. She would never again have to listen to her father's shouts and her mother's sobs.

Then she pictured herself choking and spluttering in the dirty water, of changing her mind when it was too late maybe. She shuddered and stepped back from the wall. Besides, she couldn't let her mother down like that.

She heard the purr of a high-powered engine coming slowly down the quays and stopping. Turning, she saw a long black limousine stopped at the curb on the far side of the road. An expensively-dressed man got out of the driver's seat. He seemed to heave himself up with an effort, Maura thought, but then he was at least fifty and very fat. He waddled slowly across the wide stretch of pavement towards the bank, where a pass machine was set into the wall.

Crossing the road in the direction of the Capel Street junction, Maura watched as the man inserted a card into the machine. A hood slide up and Maura saw a screen like a small television on which letters sprang up as he pressed keys beside it. Suddenly bank notes started to slide out of a slot. They were blue—twenties—a great big pile of them. Maura froze, looking at the notes as if she had been hypnotized.

The man picked them up casually and started to flick through them. There must have been ten of them at least. Two hundred pounds! Enough, Maura thought, to clear the debt to Ma Mulcahy in one fell swoop! And all she would have to do would be to snatch them from his hand! There was no-one to see her and he would never catch her. She would be up Capel Street and round the bend of Strand Street before he could waddle to the corner. She felt sick at the thought of how easy it would be.

The man must have felt her eyes on him for he turned to face her, the notes still in his hand. When he saw her he smiled as he took in the red-gold hair reaching to the skinny shoulders, the long legs in the shabby jeans.

"Hullo, my dear," he said. "How would you like to earn yourself one of these?"

Maura gave him one horrified glance and fled. Up Capel Street and into Strand Street she ran, just as she had imagined herself doing, but without the thick pile of blue bank notes that would have solved all their problems. With tears of shame and disgust stinging her eyes, she did not stop running till she was back at May's house.

May took one look at her face and closed the kitchen door quickly between them and the rest of the family.

"What happened you?" she cried.

"Oh May!" Maura whispered. "I'm so scared!"

"Is it your father?" May asked, alarmed.

Maura shook her head.

"It's me I'm scared of," she said. "I don't know what's happened to me. There was all this money, loads of it, and I almost nicked it! I mean, the man looked like he'd never miss it and we need it so bad. It would have been real easy too. He was just asking to have it nicked. And I wouldn't have felt one bit sorry for him either. I mean, he was disgusting, the way he leered at me. I know he wanted me to get into the car with him. If Michael Casey doesn't have any work for me soon I'm scared I'll do something real desperate!"

May stared at her, dumbfounded, for a second and then made up her mind.

"Hang on!" she said. "Richie has a plan to get money."

"Oh, May, that's fantastic!" Maura breathed. "Why didn't you say?"

"He only just told me," May said, "and I wasn't sure we ought do it. We'd be in trouble if the fuzz caught us. But we wouldn't be robbing anybody and it would be better than nicking things or getting into men's cars."

"I don't care what it is," Maura said. "I'll do it!"

"Only you'll have to swear not to tell anyone," May added.

"Cross my heart!" Maura promised.

"Hang on then," May said. "I'll get Richie."

"Will Mr Sullivan have work for all six of us then?" Maura asked, when Richie had told her the whole story.

"We won't say there's six of us," he told her. "Me and Whacker will collect the stuff and then divvy it up between us. We ought to shift it real quick with six of us at it. Then we can meet and pool the take and me and Whacker can bring it back to him and get our cut."

"How much do we get?" Maura asked anxiously.

"Don't know yet," Richie said. "We've to sort all that out in the morning. But Whacker will see we get a fair deal. He's smart enough like that."

So next morning, while Richie and Whacker set out for Loftus Lane, Imelda Kelly and Mickser joined May and Maura on the Square.

"I don't see what we can do till the others get back," Mickser said grumpily. Although the need for Richie and Whacker to go on their own had been explained to him, he resented being left to wait with the girls.

"They're not coming back here," May explained. "We don't want anyone seeing us with the stuff and asking awkward questions. We've to meet them in half-an-hour in the arcade at the back of the GPO and Richie says we've each to get ourselves a box to put our share of the stock in. Has anyone got a box at home?"

"What class of a box?" Imelda asked.

"Something big enough to hold a couple of dozen scarves or caps," May said.

"Like a shoe box?" suggested Mickser.

"The very thing," May agreed. "A shoe box would be great."

"We could ask in the shoe shop on the corner of Abbey Street," Imelda suggested.

"Yeah, and there's a nice girl works in that shop," May said. "I've seen her face a few times waiting for the one with the key to open up in the mornings. I wouldn't mind asking her."

So they all set off for Abbey Street.

"I don't think we should all go in," May said when they neared the corner of O'Connell Street. She was thinking that two girls on their own would look like customers, but three plus Mickser might look like a gang. "Maybe if I went because I know the girl and Imelda because it was her idea."

"That's OK," Mickser agreed. "We'll wait outside the snack bar."

The girl May remembered was in the shop all right. She was serving a stout lady sitting in the middle of a row of chairs facing the shop window. An older woman was checking the numbers on a pile of boxes and she turned her head as May and Imelda entered the shop.

"Yes," she said sharply, coming towards them. "Can I help you?"

For a second May hesitated.

"I wanted to talk to the other lady," she stammered awkwardly, but the woman took the suggestion calmly enough.

"Customers of yours, Joan," she called across to the girl. "When you're ready." Then she went back to checking boxes.

The girl turned her head for a moment and smiled at May and Imelda before sliding a black court shoe on to the right foot of the stout lady.

"She thinks we've bought shoes here," May whispered to Imelda, "and that now we're going to buy more!"

"Probably gets a cut on everything she sells, the way we will," Imelda whispered back.

"She's going to be awful mad when all we ask for is boxes!" May muttered.

"What harm, so long as we get what we came for," Imelda sniffed. "She can't nick us for just asking."

The stout lady wanted to try on the left shoe as well. Then she walked up and down for a bit and looked at herself in the mirror. Finally she decided to take the shoes. The girl went to take them off but the stout lady stopped her.

"I'll wear them," she said, handing the girl a few notes. "You can put my old ones in a bag for me."

"D'you not want the box?" the girl asked.

"Couldn't be bothered," the woman said, as Imelda and May exchanged glances. The girl left the box lying on the floor while she put the worn brown shoes into a plastic bag and rang up the money on the cash register. Then she handed the woman a receipt and a one penny piece.

"Your change," she said. Then she came across to where May and Imelda were standing.

"I'm afraid we don't want to buy anything," May whispered apologetically, before the girl could say, 'Can I help you?' "We wondered what happened to the boxes the shoes come in if the customers don't take them."

The girl laughed.

"They go into the bin," she said. "Why? Are you doing a survey or something?"

"We'd like to take the empty ones if you've no use for them," May told her.

"The bins were emptied yesterday," the girl said. "How many d'you want?"

"Four."

The girl laughed again.

"There's one there on the floor you can have for a start. I'll see if there's another three outside."

Imelda picked up the empty box with its lid from the floor beside the row of chairs.

"We'll take the good paper too," she said. "It might come in handy for something."

Then the girl came back with a little pile of boxes, stacked one on top of the other.

"Will these do you?" she asked.

"Great. Thanks!" May mumbled. "And next time I want shoes I'll try here."

The girl laughed a third time.

"Then you'd better have a card," she said, handing them a small square of cardboard with the name of the shop on it. "Don't forget now, will you? I'll be counting on you!"

Then she walked them to the door as if they were real customers.

"You don't want a bag for them?" she asked.
May shook her head.

"They'll do grand the way they are. And thanks a million!"

Waving to the other two to catch up with them, they walked up O'Connell Street towards Prince's Street and the arcade. When they got there, they waited for a while with no sign of Richie and Whacker.

"I hope nothing's gone wrong," Maura said nervously.

"What could go wrong?" scoffed Mickser.

"Maybe Ned Sullivan wouldn't give them enough for all of us," May suggested.

"Or wouldn't give us a proper cut," Maura added anxiously.

A garda and bangharda turned into the arcade from the Henry Street end and all four automatically retreated with their boxes into the doorway of Marks and Spencers.

"Hey!" the garda called after them suddenly, and Maura stopped guiltily as the others melted away inside the shop.

The bangarda stooped and picked up something from the ground. What had she found that Maura would be blamed for? Her heart thumped painfully under her T-shirt. She had heard stories of London cops framing street traders. Her father said they would even plant dope on you if they had something against you.

"One of the others dropped this," the bangharda said, holding something out to her. When Maura had the courage to look she saw it was a shop card with the name of the shoe shop written on it.

"Thanks," she mumbled, slipping it quickly into the pocket of her jeans.

She watched the foot patrol pass on down the arcade. Her heart was still thudding. For the first time she realized the dangers that lay ahead of them. If she could get into a panic over a friendly bangarda when she had nothing more incriminating than an empty shoe box, how would she feel at the sight of a hostile garda when the box was stuffed with goods for illegal selling?

4
OR DO WITHOUT

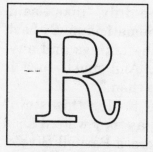ichie and Whacker had left Loftus Lane with mixed feelings. It was true that they each carried a box full of stuff for selling, but it was not the World Cup caps and scarves they had expected.

"You can't expect to get my best line from Day One," Ned Sullivan had told them when they pointed this out. "I'm only giving you a try-out till I see how you do. Shift this lot for me fast and I might try you on the caps and scarves next time."

"How much?" Whacker asked, accepting defeat on the choice of stock.

"It's dead simple," Ned Sullivan said. "Everything's a pound. Two lighters a pound. Pair of sunglasses a pound. I'm looking for salesmen, not mathematicians."

"I mean what do *we* get out of it?"

"Twenty per cent."

"That's 20p on everything we sell," Richie commented, after a second's calculations.

"Unless things have changed since I went to school," Ned remarked drily. "Like I said, I'm not looking for mathematicians. Be back here before nine with the takings and anything you fail to shift. And make sure it checks. We can divvy up then."

"I hope we'll be able to flog this stuff," Whacker said to Richie, as they waited for a break in the traffic to cross Parnell Street. "It's not going to be as easy to shift as World Cup gear."

"We gotta sell the lot," Richie told him. "Otherwise he won't give us enough for all six of us tomorrow. And if we do shift it all we'll be making good money."

"It's not that great," Whacker argued. "Not for six people working all day."

"Look at it this way," Richie said. "If we can make twenty quid a day between us we can pay off Ma Mulcahy in a couple of weeks!"

"We'd want to take a hundred quid a day for that!" Whacker cried." That's fifty pairs of sunglasses and a hundred lighters. We don't even have that many here!"

"Near enough! We've four dozen pairs of glasses and eight dozen lighters. That's £19.20 for us if we shift the lot."

"*If*!" Whacker stressed, "and it's a pretty big 'if'!"

"It's only eight dozen sales," Richie told him. "Ninety-six between the six of us. That's only sixteen each!"

"Look at, we haven't sold anything yet," Whacker pointed out. "Let's see how we get on before we start offering to buy out Michael Smurfit!"

"What kept you?" Mickser asked impatiently, as they turned into the arcade.

"Nothing," Richie told him. "It takes a while you know, sorting out the stock."

"Well," Mickser said, "the fuzz were through here while we were waiting. We'd want to move out before they come round again or they'll want to know what we're at."

"Right!" Richie nodded. "Let's head for the lane beside the Adelphi. We can talk as we go."

"What's the deal?" Mickser asked before they were even out of the arcade.

"20p a sale," Whacker told him. "Three of us sell dark glasses and three lighters."

"Bags the lighters," cried Imelda immediately.

"Me too," Mickser shouted.

"It doesn't matter who sells what," Richie told them. "Aren't we pooling the profit anyway? You can sell lighters today. You may get sunglasses tomorrow. Or we may have a different line altogether. For now May, Maura and I can do the sunglasses and Whacker lighters."

"Fair enough," Whacker agreed. "Who's taking what pitch?"

"I'm taking the bank," Richie said. "Ned Sullivan says it's a dodgy pitch so I'll do it my self for starters. Mickser can do one side of the bridge and May the other. Maura and Imelda can do either side of O'Connell Street. That way we'll have sunglasses one side of the bridge and lighters the other. Same with O'Connell Street. People selling on the bridge can do the quays as well. Outside the video shop might be good. Whacker will do Henry Street. If there's a real downpour we'll meet back in the arcade."

By now they had reached the narrow lane beside the Adelphi Cinema. Richie looked around. There was no-one in sight.

"Now, let's make this snappy," he instructed. "Hold out your boxes."

He counted out thirty two lighters from Whacker's box and put them into Mickser's. Then he did the same with Imelda's.

"Two for a pound," he said, "and don't wave the takings about! We don't want anyone putting their eye on them."

Then he counted out sixteen pairs of sunglasses from his own box for May and another sixteen for Maura.

"A pound a pair," he said, "and watch out for the fuzz."

"What happens if we sell out?"—Mickser wanted to know.

"Can't you get more off someone who hasn't?" Richie said. "You know where we'll all be. Now let's get going and mind yourselves."

"So, while Whacker went back the way they had come, the other five walked on down to O'Connell Street.

"Bags this side," Imelda said, so May and Maura crossed the road, leaving Imelda outside the Kentucky Fried Chicken. Richie wished he could have stayed with Mickser on the bridge, where the stallholders were doing a great trade in silk scarves, wallets and jewellery, but he walked on to where the portico of the Bank of Ireland jutted out beyond the busses that were parked in a line down Westmoreland Street.

As he reached the last of the shops, Richie saw a squad car come round the corner from

College Green and stop at the traffic lights in front of the bank. Between foot patrols coming along Westmoreland Street and appearing without warning around the curve from College Green, as well as coming down Grafton Street passed the railings of Trinity College opposite, he would need to have eyes in the back of his head, Richie thought, without squad cars stopping at the lights right beside him. He was only a stone's throw from Pearse Street Garda Station. No wonder Ned Sullivan had warned him it was a dodgy pitch.

Still, for that very reason he would probably have it to himself. Then he noticed something that lifted his heart. A caravan was parked near the end of the portico, selling tickets for a rock concert with a small queue in front of it. At the point where the curve of the pavement ended, leaving space inside the flow of traffic sweeping on down Westmoreland Street, a passing garda could hardly fail to see it, so it must have had permission to park there. He could work the queue and maybe hide in it if there was any trouble. He marched boldly up to the queue.

"Get your sunglasses," he said confidently. "Only a pound a pair!"

"Are they good ones?" a girl asked.

"Of course," Richie told her. "Try them for yourself," and he slipped a pair into her hand.

"How do I look?" she asked the boy beside her, when she had set them on her nose.

Before he could draw breath, Richie answered her himself.

"Smashing!" he said. "Just like Kylie Minogue."

She laughed.

"You would say that, wouldn't you? What d'you think, Sean?"

"They're OK," the boy said. "If you need sunglasses, that is!"

"Well, the ones I had got sat on last week," she said. "Can you lend me a quid?"

The boy fished around in his pocket and produced a note. Flushed with triumph, Richie slipped it into his pocket. He had made his first sale. As he did so, a man who had just joined the queue put a hand on his shoulder. Certain that he was a plainclothes detective or an off-duty cop, Richie stared back nervously.

"Give us a look," he said.

"Only a pound a pair!" Richie told him, quickly getting back his confidence as he slipped a pair from his box.

"Are they strong?" the man asked, twisting them in his hand.

Richie watched him anxiously, while he tried to stay cool. Was the man deliberately trying to break them? If one of the hinges broke no-one would buy them and Ned Sullivan would never take them back. The price would be deducted from their share of the take.

"Strong enough for the purpose they're intended for," he snapped, trying to joke and sound tough at the same time. "Not for using as worry beads."

He snatched them back and the man laughed.

"Had you worried there, hadn't I? Not quite so confident after all!"

"If you don't want the goods, don't mess them about," Richie told him. "I'm selling, not busking!"

"I'll take a pair," the man in front said, holding out a pound.

"There's a man with a nose for a bargain that knows a good thing when he sees it!" Richie said in delight, handing him the glasses and pocketing the note.

He tapped the side of his nose like a clown, and a man with an American accent laughed, holding out a pound.

"Here you are, wise guy!" he said. "I'll be back this way in the spring and if the sunglasses don't last till then you're in big trouble!"

"Right!" Richie grinned, handing over another pair. "And if I don't see you in the spring, I'll see you in the mattress!"

He was beginning to enjoy himself, he had sold three pairs already and the crack was good. Suddenly, out of the corner of his eye, he glimpsed blue uniform.

Had he been seen selling? If he had he would be pulled out of the queue. If he hadn't, he would only attract attention by running.

Clutching the box tightly under his arm, he pushed through the queue until it was between him and the garda. Then he walked quickly over to join the smaller queue which had formed in front of the PASS machine in the wall of the bank. He put the box on the ledge where the queue would hide it and leaned forward so his face would also be hidden, while he pretended to grope in his pocket for his pass card. Then he waited, his heart hammering.

* * *

Maura was finding selling on O'Connell Street hard. Hovering near the bank on the

corner of Abbey Street, she had called out
half-heartedly to a couple of passers-by, but
they had looked away and hurried on as if
she had been begging. Then the man on the
nearby newstand shouted at her angrily.

"Get away out of that or I'll have you run
out of it! You're frightening away my customers!"

Maura hurried on towards the bridge.
Then she noticed a small queue at the no 11
bus stop. Uncertainly, she wandered over to it.

"Sunglasses, only a pound!" she mumbled.

Everyone in the queue ignored her except
for one old fellow.

"Looka, love," he said, "you'll want to be a
great deal bolder than that if you're to do
business. Go on over to the next queue and
give it out to them goodo!"

Maura knew he was right. Hadn't she
heard the women crying their wares in
Moore Street all her life? She looked quickly
away at the queue over at the no 10 bus stop.
There was a young man at the tail end of it
who looked as if he wouldn't snap at her. He
was gazing into the distance towards the
bridge, away from the approaching traffic, as
if his thoughts were far away. For a second
she hesitated, nerving herself. Then she
marched boldly up to him.

"Only a pound the sunglasses," she said loudly.

He started with surprise, swinging round to face her, but then he smiled.

"D'you think I need them?" he asked.

"You were screwing up your eyes," she told him earnestly. "They say it's not good to be doing that."

"What a saleswoman!" he laughed. "How much did you say they were?"

"Only a pound," Maura repeated, holding out a pair for him to see. "They're real cheap but they're good ones."

He fumbled in his pocket and found two 50p pieces.

"Here you are then," he said. "I hope you get to keep something out of it."

Maura's face lit up. She nodded.

"Thanks," she whispered. "That's my very first sale."

A no 10 bus drew up at the stop and the man followed the people ahead of him on to the running board. As he waited for the people to pay, he turned and called back, "May it be the first of many!"

Maura smiled and watched as his bus moved off. There was no-one now at the no 11 stop either. Their bus must have come while she had been talking to the man, but she could work the bus queues further up the street. There were several near Clery's and, by the time she had tried them, there would be fresh queues for the 10 and 11. Or she could go on further to the stops beyond Parnell Street. Feeling a great deal more confident, she hurried past the newspaper stand and across Abbey Street.

* * *

Mickser was enjoying himself. None of the licensed sellers on the bridge were doing lighters, and they didn't seem to mind him joining them. He had placed himself beside two of them—tall gangling youths with Texan drawls and glasses like he wore himself— selling from boards covered in earrings and pendants.

"Look at all them Specky Four-Eyes!" shouted a little kid who passed by with her mother, pointing at them.

"What did she say?" drawled one of the Texans.

"She called us Specky Four-Eyes," Mickser told him, "on account of we all wear specs."

"Hey, Hank, how d'ya like that?" the Texan called to his companion. "I gotta remember that one!"

And from then on he would throw the odd word to Mickser any time business slacked off.

"Get your lighters! Two for a pound!" Mickser called out constantly to the steady stream of people wandering in both directions over the bridge.

Within an hour he had made four sales, but so many people passed, he decided, that even if only one in a hundred bought from him, he had a good chance of getting rid of all he had before evening. When he spotted a foot patrol he had got ready to run but his new friend told him to stand his ground.

"Brazen it out and he'll figure you're with us," he said and, as the men in blue strolled by, he had called out to Mickser, "Hey, Mac, how are you fixed for change?"

The patrol had strode on, ignoring Mickser as he made a show of fumbling in his pocket for coins.

"Thanks, cowboy," he had grinned. "Do the same for you one day!"

He was in tearing humour now. With a good-selling line and a good pitch, he was thinking of going into business on his own account, as soon as they had raised enough money to pay off Ma Mulcahy.

* * *

On the far side of the bridge, May found the going less easy. A blind man sat against the parapet of the bridge with a box on the ground in front of him, but he was not too blind to see May.

"Get to hell outa that!" he swore at her, before she had made a single sale. "What d'you think you're at, taking the bread and butter out of the mouth of a poor blind man?"

There were no licensed sellers this side of the bridge and people seemed to hurry across it instead of sauntering, as they did on Mickser's side. May thought about moving to Eden Quay. There were buses parked there, but no-one seemed to be queuing. People were going in and out of the magazine shop, but they didn't hang around. It was too early for the nearby cinema and the video place was quiet, on the outside at least.

May could see people queuing in D'Olier Street. There were bus stops there and people seemed to be hanging around in the doorways of the newsagents and café. There was traffic in and out of the Gas Company Showrooms too. She decided to wander up that way and try her luck.

* * *

Imelda was also having a slow start. With Pizzaland, Burgerland, Jasper's and the Playland ice-cream parlour, as well as the Kentucky Fried Chicken, she had thought she had bagged the best pitch, but she had found out something so obvious that she was kicking herself for not having realized it before. People ate fast food because they were in a hurry, and people in a hurry don't stop to buy from street traders. She sold a pair of lighters to a man outside the Drugstore and two more outside Eason's, but the bus stop there was a set down stop only and people never seemed to hang around when they got off the bus. She decided she might do better near the GPO. Later she could try outside the Carlton Cinema. She started to walk in the direction of the GPO.

* * *

Around the corner in Henry Street, Whacker was doing a roaring trade. Since cars were no longer allowed to drive down Henry Street, people sauntered backwards and forwards across it to look in shop windows, so he could sidle up to them and catch their attention.

"Two a pound the lighters," he called out, flicking one on and off in front of passers-by so they would notice him and see how the lighters worked every time.

"Get your lighters! Only a pound the two! Lights up at the first flick!"

"Now you look like a girl that wouldn't be satisfied with just any old flame!" he cracked to a girl in a group on their lunch break who stopped to watch him flicking his lighter on and off.

"Guaranteed to light up your life!" he teased, as she and her friend, giggling, bought a pair between the two of them.

By time he had worked his way down almost to the junction with Mary Street, he realised he had only two lighters left. Soon he would go back to O'Connell Street and see if Imelda had any to spare.

It was unlikely she would have shifted them as fast as he had.

"Get your lighters!" he called to a man and his wife who were strolling by.

"Do they work?" the man asked.

"Everyday, like a man on piece rates," Whacker joked. "Watch me carefully!" and he flicked one of his last pair on and off.

Suddenly he caught the sound of a familiar heavy measured tread. Glancing behind him he saw a pair of gardaí coming straight towards him and, in a flash, he had thrust the lighter into his pocket and melted into the crowd around the nearest doorway. They were still heading in his direction. He slipped between two women with shopping baskets and on into the store.

Edging along a counter he doubled around it to place a stand between himself and the door. Holding his breath, he peered from the far side of it. There was no sign of blue uniform in the doorway. They were not after him at all. He breathed more freely. Should he run after the man and his wife? He had had them almost hooked. It was a pity to lose them but it didn't really matter. There would be plenty more where they came from. Then a heavy hand fell on his shoulder.

"And what do you think you're doing, young fellow?"

As he spun round, the grip on his shoulder tightened into a vice. He was being held fast by the store security guard.

5
TRUST NO-ONE

ichie felt as if he had stood in the queue at the PASS machine outside the Bank of Ireland for ages, hardly daring to breath. If he had been seen selling, had he been seen disappearing into the queue? Maybe he would have done better to run. He was fast on his feet; much faster than the average beat-pounder. If a heavy hand descended on his shoulder now it would be too late to run. On the other hand, there were so many gardai in the area he might run from one pair straight into the arms of another.

The queue was moving up. In a few minutes it would be his turn at the machine. With no idea how it worked and no card, he could hardly keep up his bluff much longer. If he were caught, he would be charged in the District Court just around the corner from their house. It would kill his mother, who had always dunned it into them to stay on the right side of the law.

Suddenly he saw two burly men in blue ahead of him under the portico of the bank, moving away around the curve of the pavement into College Green. They hadn't seen him after all. And he must only have been standing in the queue for seconds, unless they had stopped to speak to someone. He almost sobbed with relief, as he broke away from the queue.

"Get your sunglasses!" he called out confidently, to a tourist with camera case strung across his shoulder. "Only a pound the sunglasses!"

There was no doubt that the world and its wife passed by under the portico of the Bank of Ireland. If he could just manage to keep dodging the fuzz it was a great pitch.

* * *

Imelda had made the same discovery about the G.P.O. Apart from the people going in and out to buy stamps or send parcels, it was a general meeting place with one or two people always hanging around outside. She sold three pairs of lighters quite quickly and gave up the idea of going on to the bus stop near the Carlton Cinema. She was doing well enough where she was. Then she realized with a shock why no-one had suggested selling there. A squad car had drawn up to the curb right opposite to her and a garda jumped out. He was heading straight for her and Imelda fled.

Round the corner into Prince's Street and through the arcade she ran, with the sound of pursuit behind her. She plunged into Henry Street, ducking in and out of the groups making their way down the middle of the road in both directions. Luckily, no car could follow her there and she was a match for any man on foot. She had the advantage of being slight and could slip in between people far more easily than a well-built man.

When she reached the junction with Denmark Street she swung right. There was a van parked outside the side door of a store and, ducking around it so it was between her and her pursuer, she ran into the store. Slowing to a walk, she moved briskly towards the most crowded counter, slipping in amongst the women waiting by the cash register and pretending to be interested in buying pop socks.

After five minutes she was sure her pursuers had given up and it would be safe to return to her pitch. Not to the GPO, she decided. It was too exposed. The bus queues would be safer. She moved away from the counter, making for the door, when suddenly she saw something that stopped her dead in her tracks. There was Whacker, her own brother, being led away by a store security man. She followed them at a safe distance until they disappeared behind a door marked "Private."

Whacker was wearing an air of injured innocence. "I done nothing!" he insisted.

"You were acting in a highly suspicious manner," the man told him. "This store is protected by closed-circuit television and you were seen behaving suspiciously at the electrical goods counter."

As he led Whacker into an inner room, Whacker began to laugh inwardly. There was nothing to fear after all. He was not being done for illegal selling. They suspected him of shop-lifting and the innocence he had pretended was real. He actually smiled as the security man took his box from him and opened it. He was glad now that all his stock was gone. It might have been embarrassing to have had to explain away thirty-two lighters, even though they could hardly have imagined he could have got that many from the counter.

The disappointment on the security man's face was comical when he found Whacker's box empty. He then proceeded to frisk Whacker energetically.

"Where did you get all this?" he asked suspiciously, eyeing the pile of one-pound notes he had pulled from Whacker's pockets.

"At work," Whacker replied self-righteously. "I was sent out to get change for three fivers in singles."

The security man counted them. There were exactly fifteen, which was not surprising, since they were the proceeds from the sale of thirty lighters.

"Aha!" cried the security man in triumph, as he found the two remaining lighters in the other pocket. "Now why would an honest person have *two* lighters?"

Whacker looked at him with round blue eyes.

"Because I just bought the two of them for a pound off a street trader as a birthday present for my da," he said.

A woman came into the room at that point. "Well," she asked, "was he counter-dipping?"

"He had these on him," the man said, holding out the two lighters.

The woman gave them a quick glance of disapproval.

"Not our stock," she said, wrinkling her nose slightly. "We don't carry those cheap lines."

"Then he's clean," the security man said reluctantly.

"I told you so," Whacker asserted. He was beginning to enjoy himself. "But you marched me off in front of all those people. Wait till I tell my da. I expect he'll sue you."

"I'm sorry," the woman said, "but you were behaving very strangely and we lose thousands of pounds from petty pilfering."

"Maybe I'll forget it this time," Whacker said grandly. "Now, if you'll excuse me, I must get back to my work."

A worried Imelda had been watching the door to the inner room from the cover of the make-up counter and now she hurried to overtake him as he swaggered out.

"What happened?" she asked as she caught up with him outside in the street, though she knew from the look on his face that things were not as bad as she had feared.

"The very girl!" he cried as he turned and saw her. "I was coming to look for you. How many lighters have you got left?"

"I only sold seven pair," Imelda admitted. "And then I had to run from the fuzz. I thought you were in trouble too."

"Not me!" Whacker grinned. "I was going to try and get something off of the store for wrongful arrest or something, but I was scared to push it while we were still trading. Old eejit thought I was shop lifting."

"I was wondering how I was going to go back and tell Mammy you'd been lifted yourself," Imelda confessed.

"I'd like to see anyone try to lift me!" Whacker boasted. "Give me a dozen of your lighters, will you? I can get rid of them easy down here."

"Have the lot," Imelda said generously, offering her box. "I don't much like this selling business and it's going to rain any minute by the look of it."

"You can surely sell three more pairs," Whacker said, thinking for the umpteenth time that Imelda didn't like doing anything unless it had an element of glamour attached to it, unlike May who would make a go of anything.

"If you can sell a dozen easy, you can sell a dozen-and-a-half," Imelda said carelessly.

"Plus the pair I've got left," Whacker said. "Oh, all right! Go on home! You'd better give me the cash for what you managed to get rid of. I knew you'd be no good at the selling. I think I'm a natural!"

"Then you needn't worry about finishing school," Imelda said tartly. "You can go right ahead and do this, can't you?"

"Oh no, I can't," Whacker cried, "except as a nixer. You know what I want is to work as a floor manager in RTE as soon as I'm old enough to apply for training."

Imelda had at least been right about the rain, Whacker thought some twenty minutes later, deciding that it was pointless trying to sell on the streets in a steady downpour. With people scurrying in and out of shops no-one was going to stop and buy. He made a few sales to people sheltering in doorways, but all the time he was working his way back towards the arcade. There would be more people sheltering there and Richie had picked it for a meeting place. When he arrived Maura was there already.

"How did you get on, kid?" he asked. He couldn't see Maura at the selling game any more than he could Imelda, though for different reasons. Maura never put on airs like Imelda, but she was shy. To his surprise she grinned at him.

"Only three left," she said, "and I'd have sold them only it went so dark. I tried saying it was bound to be sunny again tomorrow but it was no good. You can't sell sunglasses in the rain. Lighters, maybe, but not sunglasses."

"You did great!" Whacker told her. "A lot better than Imelda. She only sold seven pairs of lighters and then gave up."

"She's as well off," Maura said. "We'll do no good now!"

Mickser joined them, looking smug. He showed them his empty box.

"I was looking for Imelda to get more off of her when it started to lash," he boasted.

"You wouldn't have found her," Whacker told him. "She's gone home. I've got her stuff, what's left of it."

"There's the fuzz back again!" Maura warned in a whisper, as the garda and bangharda appeared suddenly at the Henry Street end of the arcade.

"What harm?" Mickser said. "We've as much right to shelter from the rain as anyone. They can't complain we're loitering now."

"Pity all the same," Whacker commented. "I meant to shift my last half-dozen lighters in here."

"They'll be gone in a minute," Maura told him, but Mickser shook his head.

"You wanta bet?" he grinned. "The law doesn't believe in getting itself wet, no more than anybody else!"

"Where's May?" Maura asked, worried. "She ought to be here!"

"Richie's not here yet either," Whacker pointed out.

"He's got further to come," Maura said. "May was only on the bridge, same as Mickser."

"No, she wasn't," Mickser argued. "I mean, not this long time. She must have wandered off somewhere. Maybe she tried the quays. I don't think she was doing much selling on the bridge."

"Then why isn't she here?," Maura demanded. "She can't have been selling sunglasses since the rain started."

"There's Richie now," Mickser said, as a slight and rain-sodden figure turned into the Prince's Street end of the arcade, the rain dripping from the end of a red curl on his forehead. He joined the others, shaking the rain off himself like a terrier after a swim.

"D'you mind, Redser?" Whacker complained. "If I want a shower I can go on to the street for myself. I hope it was worth getting that wet."

"Only one pair left," Richie told him. "The bank's great while there's a mobile box-office parked there. I don't know that I'd chance it without that. You need eyes in the back of your head with the amount of garda activity around. What happened May and Imelda?"

"Imelda shoved off," Whacker said. "No-one seems to know about May."

"We'd better wait for her to divvy up," Richie said, "and then me and Whacker can head off to Loftus Lane. We're not going to do much good around here now!"

"I wonder what's keeping her," May said uneasily.

"What's your hurry?" Whacker asked. "We can't sort out the cash under the eyes of the fuzz across the way. She'll be here soon enough."

But the minutes passed in fives and tens with no sign of May, until even the boys became uneasy. Had they known where she was at that moment they might have been more worried.

May had done better in D'Olier Street than on the bridge. She began by offering her sunglasses to people in the queue at the no 14 bus stop near the Gas Company offices, but an old country fellow had made a jeer of her.

"Do I look like I was on my way to the Canaries or one of them foreign places?" he had asked. "Or is it that you're thinking I might take a pair back for the heifer?"

After his bus had come and gone, however, she did manage to sell a few pairs by working the four bus stops in D'Olier Street, as well as one pair at the door of the café. Then things grew very quiet, so she crossed over into Fleet Street, where a large group of people were waiting for the 46A. She had just managed to talk a girl there into buying a pair when two men came out of the door of a newspaper office a little way up the street.

"Look!" she heard one of them say, but she was too busy getting the money for the glasses to take note of them until she heard an unmistakable click. Swinging round, she saw that one of them had a camera focussed on herself. As the photographer turned away, she hurried after him.

"Hey, mister!" she gasped breathlessly. "You took a snap of me, didn't you?"

"I did," the photographer nodded, smiling. He seemed to expect May to be delighted about it. "It looked good too. How would you like to see a picture of yourself on the paper?"

"Ah no!" May cried. "You mustn't put it on the paper. You'll get me into awful trouble. I'm not supposed to be doing this at all!"

"Don't worry!" the man laughed. "I won't use your name. But that photo might just win me a prize in the Photographer of the Year awards. If you could only see the expression on your face as you held out the sunglasses to the queue!"

"I think the judges might go for it," the other man agreed. "It's good social comment too. Dublin's getting like Mexico City these days, between people begging with babies and children selling in the streets."

"But you don't understand," May pleaded. "We've no license to sell, and if the papers start writing about us there'll be a fuss. Then the guards will be twice as bad chasing after us. And we have to keep selling to get enough money to pay back the moneylender."

"Do I smell a story?" the man without a camera said. "This could be interesting. Why don't we all go and have a cup of coffee and talk about it?"

May shook her head.

"If you put that picture on the paper you'll make trouble for us all."

The man looked thoughtfully at her for a moment. He was older than the photographer and balding, but he looked more understanding. There was more hope of sympathy from Old Baldy Conscience, May thought.

"Tell you what," he said finally. "Come across to Bewley's with us and tell us your story. If you can convince us that using the photo would really do you harm, maybe we won't use it. But perhaps we can convince you that it could help."

"I can't!" May said stubbornly. "I've to sell the rest of these."

"How many have you got?"

May showed him the contents of her box, and he counted the ten pairs of sunglasses.

"How much?" he asked.

"Only a pound a pair," May told him eagerly, seeing him for the first time as a potential customer.

"If I buy the lot, will you talk to us?"

It was very tempting. It might take hours to make ten sales. She might not even manage to sell all of them. The sky was beginning to darken and no-one would buy sunglasses when it was like that. She couldn't come to much harm in Bewley's, she thought, and she could be careful what she told them. She could maybe get them to promise not to use the photo.

Probably no-one in the square would see it, if they did. It was the evening papers they bought. They were cheaper, but then you never could tell who might see a paper. Old Danny might see it in the Public Library. He read everything, though she could always ask him not to tell. It was the gossipy old ones like Mrs Doyle who would be dangerous. Supposing she saw it at the chipper or wrapped around a take-away? Or someone might give it to Mr Doyle to put under his paint pots. Mrs Doyle might even notice it, sticking out of a litter bin near the Legal Eagle, where one of the men out of the Four Courts had thrown it. It wasn't very likely, but you never could tell.

Even if no-one in the Square to to hear about it, the fuzz would. And if people started fussing about cleaning up the streets, selling without a licence could become impossible until the fuss died down again. And if they had to stop selling, how would they ever get the money to pay off Ma Mulcahy? The photo would be dangerous. She was sure of it. She must talk Old Baldy Conscience out of using it.

"OK," she said. "Give me the ten pounds and I'll come. Only to Bewley's, mind.

"Done!" Baldy Conscience said, smiling, as he handed her a crisp ten-pound note.

In Bewley's, he found a table and told May and the photographer to sit at it. Then he went across to the self-service counter for the coffees and, when he returned, he had a plate of cakes and cream buns that made May's eyes pop out of her head.

"Work away at those," he told her, as he set the plate down in front of her.

He was making it very hard for her to refuse to tell him everything he wanted to know, May thought. Maybe it might be better not to eat the buns. Then she wouldn't feel mean about not telling him everything, but they looked so deadly, with the cream oozing out of them.

"Anyway," she reasoned, "he's already paid for them now and it's not as if I'd asked for them. It's his own fault!"

Having arrived at this satisfactory conclusion, she wasted no more time but bit into one of the buns and let the cream melt slowly in her mouth.

"Now," Baldy Conscience said, when her mouth was no longer full, "what's all this about moneylenders? Is your family in a lot of debt?"

"Not mine," May told him, "a friend's," hastily adding, "but she wouldn't want you writing about it on the paper."

"You don't need to tell me her name or where she lives," he said quickly. "I only want to know how much was borrowed and what it was wanted for."

"I suppose that might be OK," May agreed cautiously. After all, if she gave him no names and never mentioned the Square it could be anybody. And he had bought all her stock as well as the cream buns.

"Maybe you could just say someone's mammy borrowed £200 for things for the Christmas," she suggested.

"Two hundred," Baldy Conscience repeated, writing on a little pad he had taken from his pocket. "Is that all?"

"But it's £260 that has to be paid back!" May cried, stung at the way he was dismissing it as something small and unimportant. "And that's an awful lot when your da's only drawing the assistance and your mammy only has what she can make at the contract cleaning!"

Baldy Conscience scribbled away furiously on his little pad.

"And is the moneylender putting a lot of pressure on her mother to pay?" he asked.

"She has the children's allowance book kept," May said, "and she says she'll talk to her da if all the money isn't paid back soon."

"Would that matter?" Baldy Conscience asked casually, continuing to write.

"Of course it matters," May shouted angrily. "She's scared of what he'll do if he finds out. He gets awful cross sometimes when he's been drinking."

"So what's the mother doing about it?" Baldy Conscience enquired and again May felt he was criticising Mrs Reilly and making light of her problem at the same time.

"She's eating nothing only bread and marge most of the time to save money," May cried indignantly, "and pawning her good coat and her wedding ring and everything so as to keep paying the sixteen pound a week."

Baldy Conscience finished writing and smiled.

"Thanks," he said. "You told that very well. It's a good story."

"But you won't put my photo on the paper?" May asked anxiously.

"You wouldn't want to stop Sean there using it, surely? Not when it might win him the competition?"

"But the guards will be at us worse than ever if he does!" May cried. "And if they caught us Mammy'd never over it! She'd have calliptions if she knew we were selling on the streets and us with no licence! And even if the guards can't catch us at it they'd keep running us so we'd never make enough to pay what's owing!"

May caught Baldy Conscience by the sleeve of his jacket in her desperation. She felt that now he had his story he was no longer interested. He would put her photo on the paper no matter what she said.

Why had she told him so much? She realized now that she had been crazy! She had ruined everything for the sake of ten pounds and three cream buns, and Maura and the others would never forgive her.

6
A SHADOW OF DOUBT

'm going to look for May," Maura said, after a quarter-of-an-hour had passed and there was still no sign of her.

"You're crazy!" Whacker told her. "You'll be washed out of it. It's lashing out of the heavens like there was a leak in the plumbing. You don't think May's standing out on the street trying to sell in this, do you? She'll have taken shelter inside somewhere."

"If she doesn't turn up when the rain eases off I'll go looking for her myself," Richie said. "You can..."

But he was interrupted by a shout from Mickser. "Will you look at what's coming, cool as you please!"

Spinning round, Maura saw May entering the arcade and, though the rain was still hopping off the pavement behind her, her clothes seemed as dry as when she left home.

"Thanks be to God!" Maura cried, running to meet her. "You had me real worried. What happened you?"

"I'm sorry," May apologized. "I didn't know it was raining till I got out of Bewley's. Were you waiting long?"

"Only a half-hour," Richie said with sarcasm, "and you in Bewley's no less! You weren't selling in there, were you!"

"In a way I was," May argued. "Look!"

She handed him a crisp ten pound note and six battered singles.

"You sold the lot!" Richie cried in amazement. "That's more than I did though I've only the two pairs left!"

"Watch it, Redser!" Whacker warned. "You're getting quare looks from across the way. Let's keep the loot out of sight till we're away from prying eyes!"

"True for you," Richie said, shoving the notes into his pocket. "Let's cut across to Moore Street. There'll be no-one to mind us there."

The heavy rain had scattered the crowds into shops and shop doorways, so Henry Street was almost deserted as they scuttled across it and took refuge under the arcade at the back of the Ilac Centre. There, between the racks of men's shoes outside Jordan's Shoe Shop and screened from the street by vegetable stalls, they could do their business unseen.

"Right," Richie ordered. "We'll take the stuff back the way it came. All sunglasses not sold into my box and all lighters into Whacker's."

In no time, five pairs of sunglasses lay side-by-side in Richie's box and ten lighters in Whacker's. Richie did some rapid mental arithmetic.

"Four dozen pairs of glasses we started with, less five is forty-three. That's forty-three quid we should have between May, Maura and myself. Let's have it!"

"I gave you mine!" May said quietly.

She wasn't her usual bouncy self, Maura thought. What had happened to make her go so quiet? And why were her clothes dry? Even if she had been in Bewley's she should have been soaked on the walk from West-moreland Street. And what had taken her into Bewley's anyway? It couldn't have been to shelter from the rain, because she had said she didn't know it was raining till she came out. It was very odd.

"May," she began, "I don't understand why..."

But Richie cut her short.

"Will you shut-up till we have this done? I want your lids."

Maura took the bundle of single notes from the pocket of her jeans and Richie counted them.

"Thirteen quid from Maura, sixteen from May and fourteen of mine, makes forty-three quid all told. That checks. Now, lighters!"

"That's easy counted," Whacker cut in. "I'd eight dozen of them, making ninety-six, less ten not sold. Two for a quid means we should have forty-three, same as for the sunglasses. Between me and Imelda I got twenty-seven quid..."

"And here's your other sixteen," Mickser finished for him, handing over the contents of his pocket.

"Eighty-six quid!" Richie cried in triumph. "Eighty-six quid in spite of the rain. We done great!"

"And what do we get out of it?" asked Mickser. Richie and Whacker seemed to fancy themselves at calculation, so let them do the work.

"Easy!" Whacker boasted again. "We get twenty per cent. Ten per cent of eighty-six quid is eighty pound sixty and twice that is seventeen twenty! Not bad!"

"More than Mammy has to give Ma Mulcahy in a week!" Maura cried delightedly.

"Then we could split the extra between us," suggested Mickser.

"That's stupid!" Richie told him. "We'd only get a few pence each for sweets or crisps. It's all to be kept to pay off Ma Mulcahy."

"Right on, Redser!" Whacker agreed. "By the end of the week we could near pay off half what's owing."

"No!" May cried suddenly. "I know what we should do with it!"

Maura looked at her in amazement. She had suddenly come to life again and her eyes burned as if a fire had been lit inside her.

"We have to take the extra money to the Credit Union in Beresford Street," May cried. "Old Danny Noonan told me about it. He said if you gave them a pound they'd make you a member and then they'd look after you for the rest of your life, no matter what. So we can give the sixteen pound to Ma Mulcahy and the one pound twenty to the Credit Union to make Mrs Reilly a member."

"I'd rather get Mammy's wedding ring back out of the pawn," Maura said, but May shook her head vigorously.

"You can do that with the money we get tomorrow or the next day," she said. "The most important thing is the Credit Union. Danny made me promise I'd give them the first pound I ever earned for myself, so now we can give them the first pound we got from the street selling."

"We can talk about that tonight," Whacker said. "Let's get the money first."

"Can't we take it out of what we've got here?" Mickser suggested, but Richie was firm.

"Whacker and me have to go back to Ned Sullivan and divvy up. If he thinks we're maybe on the fiddle he won't get us any more stock. The rest of yous can go home."

The downpour had changed to a steady drizzle as Richie and Whacker went on up Moore Street and the girls turned back into Henry Street, heading for the Square. Mickser had gone off on some business of his own and Maura was glad of it. It would give her a chance to talk to May without Imelda or the boys being around.

"How come you didn't get wet before?" she began cautiously.

"I was left back by car," May told her. "The old baldy fellow I was with in Bewley's drove me."

"You went to Bewley's with some dirty old man!" Maura screamed in horror. "Oh, May, how could you?"

"Ah no," May said. "It wasn't like that at all. The photographer that was with him took a snap of me and they wanted to put it on the papers."

"Like you were a model!" Maura gasped. "Will they pay you for using it?"

"Ah no, it's not like that," May repeated. "they work for the papers and they want to write about us selling and that."

"But they can't!" Maura went white. "If Da got to hear of it he'd murder me and Mammy too for not knowing about it and stopping me!"

"They won't put names on anyone," May said. "They can't, 'cos I didn't give them any."

"It's awful risky," Maura said. "Oh, May, I wish you hadn't done it."

"So do I," May said. "But he bought ten pairs of sunglasses off of me. If he hadn't we wouldn't have the extra for the Credit Union. If we can pay that I won't be sorry I did it."

Meanwhile, Richie and Whacker were knocking on the door of Ned Sullivan's house in the alley of Loftus Lane. The door was opened by an angular woman with her hair scraped back off her head into a bun.

"What d'you want?" she asked suspiciously.

"Is Ned in?" Whacker asked. "We been selling for him."

"He's in his office," she snapped, jerking her thumb towards the garage. "Just bang on the door there and don't ever come calling to the house annoying me again."

Then she slammed the door shut again.

"Nice lady!" commented Whacker sarcastically.

"A real charmer," Richie agreed, as he hammered on the green garage door.

Ned unlocked the door and they picked their way between a stack of boxes and cartons that Richie decided were full of things for selling. Beside them was the van they had seen Ned unloading the day before while, at the back, was a partitioned cubicle with papers and exercise books and a telephone on a little shelf. Beside the phone was a high stool which looked as if it had been lifted from its rightful place beside some bar counter and, on the stool sat a thickset man with black hair and sallow skin.

"Washed out of it, were you?" Ned asked, looking at the two boys with their wet hair clinging to their heads and the rain dripping from the bottoms of their jeans.

"It wasn't much good going on," Richie said. "No-one was buying once the rain started."

"Can't be helped so," Ned said. "Did you manage to shift anything before it came down?"

"Sure. Show him what's left, Whacker."

With a flourish, the boys set their boxes down on top of the stacked cartons and removed the lids.

"Is that all?" Ned asked.

He was clearly surprised. It had been a short day, yet these two managed to sell eighty-six lighters and forty-three pairs of sunglasses, for he was not to know they were only part of a team.

"That's all," Whacker said casually.

"You got eighty-six quid for me, lads?"

Richie nodded, counting it carefully into Ned's palm.

"And we want seventeen pound twenty back," he said.

Ned grinned and took a twenty pence piece from his pocket.

"You got it!" he said, counting seventeen single notes back into Richie's eager hand. "I was wrong about you two," he admitted. "You did OK. If you want World Cup gear tomorrow you can have it."

"Thanks," Whacker said smoothly. "We'll take it."

"The new stock's not unpacked yet. There'd be no sense anyway in carting it hither and yon in the rain. Call down tomorrow morning and I'll fix you up."

Richie gave him a nod of thanks.

"Right," he said. "See you!"

He turned on his heel and went with Whacker to the door. It had been smooth as silk. They were laughing. With his hand on the door handle, they heard Ned suddenly call after them:"Hang on a minute, lads. I almost forgot. There's someone wants to see you!"

They turned in surprise to see the black-haired man coming towards them across the garage floor. Now they realized for the first time how big he was. Sitting on the stool behind the partition, only the huge shoulders had been visible. Now they found themselves facing a man well over six foot in height, but so solidly built that you wouldn't realize how tall he was until he was towering over you.

"I hear you were there when Tony got hit!" he said. "Is that right?"

Richie would have loved to deny it. He had no idea who this giant was, but whatever his interest it would be safer to know nothing. On the other hand, Ned knew the truth. After all, that was how they got Tony's job. It would be foolish to try to hide it.

"That's right," he admitted reluctantly.

"D'you know the guards are looking for witnesses?"

"Is that right?" Richie replied cautiously.

He was playing for time. The big guy might be anxious for them to help the gardaí with their enquiries. On the other hand, he might be determined to make sure they kept their mouths shut. The one sure thing was that he was no man to cross. It would be wise not to show their hand until he had shown his.

"They say there was a crowd around the ambulance when they arrived," he continued, "but all of them swore they had arrived on the scene too late to see anything."

"We were gone before the fuzz turned up," Whacker said quickly.

"We called the ambulance right enough, but as soon as we saw Tony safely on to the stretcher, we split."

"Thanks for getting help," the big man said shortly. "Now make a right job of it and help him some more."

That seemed to show whose side he was on, Richie thought, but he was still cautious.

"You're a friend of Tony's so?" he asked.

"His father. That boy's going to be in hospital for a while. He's several ribs cracked and I want to know who's responsible. I want to know what bastard could do that to my son and not even stop to find out is he alive or dead!"

"Ah, well," Whacker put in hastily, "I'm afraid we can't help you there. I never seen the driver in my life."

"But you know what he looked like?"

"A young lad," Richie told him," about the same age as Tony. And there was another even younger with him. Joy-riders, by the look of them. Either that or they were robbing the car."

"And what class of a car was it?"

"A blue Ford Granada," Whacker said promptly. "The 1988 two-litre GL."

"You didn't happen to notice the registration number?"

"Sure," Whacker told him, "88 D 173, but if the car was robbed that's not going to help much."

"That's for the guards to worry about," the big man said, "but I'll tell you this much: if I lay my hands on them that did it they'll be longer in hospital than Tony. And the same goes for anyone that helps them or stops me getting a hold of them."

Richie felt a prickly sensation at the back of his neck and the sweat broke out on his forehead. He was in a great hurry to make it clear that neither Whacker nor he could be classed amongst them.

"What d'you want us to do?" he asked.

"What any witness is supposed to do by law: go to the guards and tell them all you know!"

"We'll do that so," Richie told him, "won't we, Whacker?"

Whacker nodded. He had no wish to test the punching power of those great fists.

"And don't delay about it either," the big man said. "I want compensation out of someone for this if it's the last thing they do and I'll not be denied for lack of witnesses. Remember, you owe Tony for letting you sell in his place."

"Oh, we do," Whacker said, "and we're sorry he's hurt so bad, aren't we, Richie?"

"We are," Richie agreed with emphasis, "and we hope he'll be better real soon."

"The best cure he could have would be news of a decent bit of compensation coming his way," his father told them, "so, if I was you, I'd go straight to the guards."

Both boys nodded vigorously to show their eagerness to do as he had suggested.

"Right so," he said. "I'll tell Tony he can stop worrying because his friends are doing their best for him. And it's well they should because if they don't it isn't friends they are at all. And those that aren't friends are enemies and an enemy of Tony's is an enemy of mine."

He glanced around him as if looking for something and then picked up an iron bar that was lying against the wall of the garage. Facing the boys, he held it lightly between his two hands. Suddenly the two fists clenched, the great chest expanded, the muscles swelled in the sinewy arms, the strong jaw tightened and, in seconds, the thick bar was a twisted, useless piece of scrap. He tossed it aside contemptuously.

"That's what I do to people who try to fool me," he said. "I'd remember that if I was you, because I'll always know how to find you."

The boys nodded dumbly. Even Whacker's quick tongue seemed to have dried up inside his mouth. Then they hurried from the door and down the lane as if the devil himself were after them.

Crossing Capel Street, Richie glanced back over his shoulder as if he half-expected to see a giant figure looming up behind them. Whacker laughed.

"Where d'you leave Tiny Tim?" he cracked.

It was as if the further they got from Loftus Lane, the more his wit came back to him.

"It's not funny," Richie said. "What are we going to do?"

"Go to the Bridewell and talk to whoever's on duty, I suppose," Whacker replied. "It's not much out of the way."

"But we can't!" Richie cried. "The last thing we want is to tangle with the fuzz. We don't want to be selling around town and our faces as well known as if we were up in the District Court every day of the week!"

"I'd sooner that," Whacker retorted, "than be crushed to pulp like that iron bar back there."

"Me, too!" Richie agreed, "but it's not just us. It's Maire and the rest of them. I mean, we did great today. We can't sabotage the whole operation!"

"We got no choice!" Whacker said grimly. "The others can't sell without us. We're the contact with Ned Sullivan. They won't do much selling with the two of us wrapped up like mummies above in Cappagh."

"But can you not find some way out of it?" Richie asked. "The way Tiny Tim would *think* we'd done what he asked?"

They had reached the corner of the lane by now and Whacker stopped and stared at Richie as if he were out of his mind.

"I thought you'd have more cop on than that, Redser!" he said. "You don't fool about with the likes of Tiny Tim. We go to the fuzz at the Bridewell, tell them exactly what we told him, no more, no less. They won't take our prints or paste our mugshots up on the wall for that! And they can't pull anyone in for it either, because all we can identify is a stolen car."

"They'll want us to identify the driver," Richie said.

"What harm? We'll say we can't. We never seen him before or since and that's not a word of a lie. I was too busy looking at the car to notice the driver."

"But I'd know him anywhere," Richie argued. "He'd a white, pasty class of a face and real yellowy hair."

"Well," Whacker said, "if I was you I'd keep that to myself, seeing as how you never mentioned it to Tiny Tim. Not that I'd put myself out to protect a stranger. Still, I'm not for informing on anyone either if I can help myself. But if we finger someone we'll be in and out of the station and the court giving evidence and we'd end up as well known as a begging ass.

"But if they ask me...," Richie began, but Whacker interrupted him.

"Forget it!" he said. "Let me do the talking. I'll say we only saw the car and it was going fast. You couldn't have seen the driver that clearly. If you were to set eyes on him this minute you mightn't know him at all."

To his amazement, Richie's response was a sort of strangled cry. He was staring over Whacker's left shoulder and his eyes were almost popping out of his head. Whacker turned to see what he was looking at, but it was only Jemmo Mulcahy coming down the lane. Then he saw that there was someone with him. It was a lad of about the same age with a white pasty face and real yellowy hair.

7
SPIN

ichie was so stunned that Whacker had to shake him by the shoulder and hurry him away before Jemmo noticed the way he was staring. Only when they reached Chancery Street did Whacker allow him to pause for long enough to get his breath back.

"You were right!" Richie gasped, as soon as he was able to speak. "The car *was* heading straight for the lane when it hit Tony. That means the Mulcahys are mixed up in it too. We can't go to the Bridewell now!"

"I can!" Whacker said. "Just leave it to me. I swear I never got a proper look at the driver! And I don't care who Jemmo was with. I never seen him before in my life. If you want to go on home that's your business, but Tiny Tim knows we were together and he'd think it odd if I turned up by meself. Sooner or later someone's going to come looking for you and I hope for your sake it's only the fuzz!"

So, in the end, Richie went with him to the Garda Station at the back of the Four Courts, beside the gate leading to the Bridewell and the District Courts.

"I hear you're looking for witnesses to a hit and run in Mary Street around eight last night," Whacker began briskly. "There was a young lad knocked down and injured."

"That's right." The man on the desk opened a big book lying close to his elbow. "Were you there?"

"I was," Whacker answered helpfully, "and I seen the whole thing. Me and Richie here were coming from the Carlton when it happened."

"And what's your name?"

Whacker told him his name and address and the garda wrote them down carefully in his big book. Then he turned to Richie but, before he had time to ask, Whacker had told his name and address too.

"Now," the garda said, as he finished writing, "will you tell me what you saw?"

Whacker told him in detail, describing where they were standing, how the car came screaming passed them and hit Tony as he was crossing the road ahead of them and plunged on across Capel Street without stopping. He also described the car.

"I couldn't tell you what the driver looked like," he concluded, "only that he seemed youngish. I was too busy making a note of the registration number."

The garda seemed impressed.

"Sergeant O'Brien will be very pleased," he said and then, turning to Richie, "and did you see all this too?"

"I did," Richie said, "though it was Whacker took note of the car number."

"And is there anything else you can add to what he has told me?"

"Only that there was a second person in the car, between me and the driver. He was dark, I think, and not a lot older than me, but I couldn't be sure. They were going too fast."

"Good lads!" The garda finished his notes and spoke with finality. "We may need you to say all that again in court, but if so someone will call up to you nearer the time."

The interview was clearly at an end. Whacker gave a nod of farewell, tugged

Richie's arm, and the two of them hurried out of the door and back down the steps on to the street. Richie breathed a sigh of relief.

"It was a pushover," Whacker commented, "and you did great! You didn't even have to lie! Of course the passenger was on our side of the car. It would have been near impossible to see the driver only for we looked back as he came around the corner. We're in the clear. We..."

He stopped dead as Richie suddenly gripped him by the shoulder. Following the direction of Richie's gaze, Whacker saw Patser Mulcahy. He was standing sheltering under the overhang of the Eastern Health Board Offices, watching them.

"How long was he there?" Whacker muttered, as they hurriedly crossed the road in the direction of the Square.

"Long enough to know where we've been," Richie replied softly, "and he didn't look one bit friendly!"

"He can't know what we were at," Whacker reassured him. "How's he to know we saw the accident?"

"Well," Richie said, "I hope he never finds out. If all the Mulcahys are out to get us, it would be near as bad as Tiny Tim!"

"That's where you and I differ!" Whacker argued. "I'll fight my corner with the best of them, but I'm not taking on Tiny Tim. That man has sledgehammers instead of fists!"

He said the same thing to Mickser when they all met up again in the Square, after the rain had eased off.

"That's all fine and dandy," Mickser said, "but it won't make selling easier. Running's no good once your face is known to the fuzz. We'd get home and find them sitting outside the door in a squad car."

"What were they supposed to do," argued May hotly. "Get themselves smashed up just to make life easier for you? Besides, that poor lad that was knocked down deserves his compensation. It's not right he should have to suffer because everyone fights shy of the rozzers."

Imelda, who was back now the hard part was over, nodded in agreement.

"Anyways," she said, "people shouldn't be let drive into someone and get away with it. Good enough for the driver if he's caught!"

"I'm not bothered about the driver," Richie told her, "but Jemmo and Patser Mulcahy are in it too. You don't shop your neighbours!"

"Who's talking about shopping anyone?"

Whacker demanded angrily. "We did no such a thing. We told the fuzz nothing about the lane and the number plate switching, and we didn't give him a description of the driver. Now let's forget it and give Maura the money."

"That's only fantastic!" Maura cried as Richie handed over the seventeen pound twenty. "Thanks a million, all of you. Mammy won't believe her eyes when she sees it!"

"I'd like to see her face when you give it to her," Mickser said, but Maura became anxious at that.

"I don't want any of yous there when I do," she told them. "She doesn't know I told you and she wouldn't be one bit happy about it."

"I was only joking," Mickser assured her and, although they all went across the Square as far as Maura's house, they waited outside while she went in with the money.

Her mother was in the kitchen, bent over a pile of ironing on the table.

"Where were you all day?" she asked irritably, as Maura came into the kitchen. "I wanted you to press a couple of shirts for your father."

"I'll tell you in a minute," Maura said. "First, you must close your eyes."

"I've no time now for playing games," her mother said shortly. "I've to leave for work in less than an hour. Having all this to do on my own has put me back. If you're not let go cleaning any more the least you can do is to give me a hand with things at home."

"Leave them," Maura told her. "I'll finish them later. Sit down and I'll put the kettle on for a cup of tea."

Exhausted, her mother slumped down at the table and put her head in her two hands, closing her eyes more from weariness than because of Maura's instructions. The minute she did so, Maura slipped the money on to the table between her two elbows. When Mrs Reilly opened her eyes again, the first thing she saw was the little pile of notes under the 20p piece.

"Glory be to God, child!" she cried, "were you out robbing a bank?"

Maura shook her head, half-laughing, half-crying.

"It was hard-earned, Mammy, every bit of it," she said, "but with a bit of luck we'll maybe have as much every day."

"You got a job!" her mother cried in delight. "You got a job and you never even told me. And isn't it a grand job that pays more than three pounds an hour and you still under age?"

Maura would have liked to let her go on believing that, but it would only cause more trouble in the end. She shook her head.

"It wasn't only me that earned it," she explained. "Richie and May and Whacker and the rest of them helped get it. We're working together as a team."

"Then it's not right for us to have it all!"

Tired though her mother was, she snatched up the money and held it out to Maura. "Give the others back their share!" she ordered.

"But they want us to have it," Maura argued, gently pushing her mother's out-stretched hand away from her. "That's why Richie organized the whole thing."

"I don't care what they want!" her mother cried angrily, again thrusting the money at Maura. "We may have fallen low in this house, but we're not yet beggars!"

"No-one's thinking we are, Mammy", Maura said soothingly, "but can't we pay them back as soon as we're on our feet again? This will pay Ma Mulcahy for the week and get back the allowance book. What we get tomorrow can be for getting your things back out of the pawn, the way me Da will never know what happened them. Then, if we do as well for the next couple of weeks you can pay off the rest of the loan."

Maura finished triumphantly but, instead of looking pleased, her mother sprang to her feet, with tears of shame in her eyes.

"So the Byrnes and the Kellys and the Dolans and every other Tom, Dick and Harry in the Square know our business!" she cried. "I never thought the day would come that my own daughter would let her family down before the whole world the like of that!"

"Ah, no, Mammy!" Maura pleaded. "Nobody knows anything only May and Richie and Whacker and Imelda and Mickser and they'd never tell. I didn't mean anyone only May to know, and I told her because I tell her everything. But then we needed the others to help us get the money. Please don't make me take it back! They'd be desperate hurt after all the trouble and we do need it awful bad!"

"D'you think I don't know that?" her mother said, and the question ended in a sound like a sob.

"Then *please* take it to Ma Mulcahy!" Maura begged. "If you don't, all the trouble they went to will be gone to waste. The minute we're clear of the mess we're in, we can pay back the others some way. I could easy do it myself if I only get a job."

Her mother hesitated a moment and then put the money back down on the table.

"You're a good girl, Maura," she said. "I'm sorry I bad-mouthed you. I'll go and see Ma the minute I get back from the cleaning."

Maura flung her arms around her mother and hugged her.

"That's great, Mammy. Things are going to be better from this out, you'll see."

Then she heard the sound of the kitchen door opening and, before she could even loose her grip on her mother, heard her father's voice behind her.

"There's a sight for sore eyes and me tramping the city all day without even the price of a pint!"

Turning, she saw to her horror her father take some of the notes from the little pile on the table.

"No, Da! she screamed. "please! Those are for..."

She broke off as she remembered that Ma Mulcahy's name must never be mentioned in front of her father.

"For what?" her father asked, but he did not even wait for an answer.

"Isn't it only the lend of a loan, I want, anyways? Just for a wet in Flynn's. Can't I pay you back on Tuesday, when I get the labour allowance money?"

Even as he said it, Maura knew it would never happen. Wasn't it hard enough to get money for the groceries off him every week, without any extra? As he started for the kitchen door, Mrs Reilly ran after him, clutching at his arm.

"Please, Jack!," she begged him. "That's not ours! It belongs to the childer. They're after working all day for it, the Byrnes and the Kellys and..."

She got no further, for her husband thrust her aside impatiently, trying to close the kitchen door on her as he covered the little hallway in three strides.

"I tell you, it's only a loan!" he said, opening the front door.

Mrs Reilly recovered her balance and ran after him again, sobbing and trying to hold him back in the doorway.

"D'you want the neighbours to see you, you bitch!" he snarled at her. "Have you no shame? Trying to disgrace your husband before the world!"

With all his strength, he flung her from him again, so that she fell backwards into the hallway. Then he slammed the front door behind him cutting off the sound of her sobbing and Maura's cry of despair.

8
SPOUT

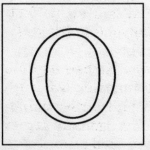utside in the Square, Patchie had found his master and friends. Bounding up to them, he pestered each member of the group in turn, until Richie finally gave in and found a stick suitable for throwing. While Patchie retrieved this and then pestered for it to be thrown once more, Mickser continued his argument about the giving of evidence to the guards.

"I hope," he told Richie and Whacker, "yous realize that, if there's any trouble with the fuzz, yous are on your own. I mean, they don't know me, do they?"

"Some friend you are!" May cried indignantly. "And how much selling would you ever have done only for Richie and Whacker getting the stuff for you to sell?"

"I dunno," Imelda said thoughtfully. "What Mickser says makes sense. There's no need for all of us to land in the soup because one of us is nicked."

"Fair enough," Richie agreed, picking up the stick that Patchie had laid at his feet. "We'll make it a rule. If anyone's nicked no-one else knows anything about it."

Patchie gave a shrill yap. He had no time for all this talk when his master was supposed to be playing with him. Absentmindedly, Richie flung the stick diagonally across the square and Patchie bounded after it.

"Mammy's never going to believe that," May pointed out.

"Don't mind her!" Mickser said. "It's the fuzz I'm talking about. If…"

"Hold it, Mickser!" Whacker cut in quickly. "Here comes Mr Reilly!"

At once they all edged further from the house, pretending to be conscious only of Patchie. He had brought back the stick but was refusing to drop it, teasing Richie by offering it to him and then bounding away each time he tried to take it. Seizing on the distraction, Richie grabbed the stick, and tried to wrest it from him, but Patchie refused to let go and a tug-of-war began.

Growling fiercely, as if Richie were his worst enemy instead of his adored master, he shook the stick like a rat, trying to twist it out of Richie's hand.

"A tug of war!" Mickser shouted, just as Mr Reilly reached his front door. "Try and drag him over the line, Patchie!" and he marked a line on the ground with the heel of his shoe.

Now Richie was growling too, imitating the ferocious noises Patchie was making as the two of them tussled for possession of the stick.

"Patchie's winning!" May laughed. "Go on, Patchie! Rats! Get 'em!"

"Isn't anybody on my side?" Richie complained, digging his heels in and tugging harder than ever. Suddenly Patchie let go of the stick and Richie fell flat on his back, the stick still in his hand. While everyone was still laughing at Richie, the door of Reilly's suddenly burst open. In the open doorway, they saw Mr Reilly struggling to free himself from Mrs Reilly's clinging hands.

Richie scrambled to his feet, as they caught a glimpse of Maura in the background.

"Please, Da, give it back!" she screamed.

With one accord, the others moved forward until they formed a little half-circle in front of the door. Suddenly Mr Reilly freed himself from his wife's grip, flinging her to the floor behind him and slamming the door. Then, turning, he found himself facing the little group of silent onlookers.

"Out of my way!" he snarled.

Nobody moved. They just stood silently, looking at him.

"Out of my way!" he repeated, pushing May roughly aside.

Richie was dimly conscious of Patchie tugging at the leg of his jeans. He had returned to the attack on the stick, which Richie was still holding. Reminded of it, he suddenly flung it in front of Mr Reilly. Hurling himself after it, Patchie scrabbled in between Mr Reilly's feet, tripping him up, so that he stumbled foolishly against the wall. Stopped in his tracks, Mr Reilly found the little group had once more closed in around him. He didn't know how much they had seen, but suddenly he remembered that his wife had said the money was theirs. He felt awkward and ashamed.

"Look at!" he said, "I was only codding, but there's some can't take a joke!"

He put his hand into his pocket and held out the fistful of notes. Whacker snapped them up smartly and put them into his own pocket.

"Thanks, Mr Reilly," he said. "I'm game for a laugh any time."

Mr Reilly looked at him for a second. Then he hurried away across the Square. Whacker went straight to the door of Reilly's and knocked. There was a long pause. Then it was opened by Maura.

"We got the money," Whacker told her. "Are yous all right?"

"Thanks be to God!" Maura said. "You'd better come in." So they all trooped in to the kitchen while she closed the door quickly behind them.

Mrs Reilly was slumped in a chair, her eyes closed and her face pale. She had one hand to her head and a thin trickle of blood ran down her fingers.

"She keeps saying she has to go to work," Maura said, "but I'm scared she's hurted bad."

"Are you all right, Mrs Reilly?" May asked, gently taking her hand away from her face to show a cut above her left eye.

"I'll be grand in a minute," she said, "soon as I've had a cup of tea."

"Maybe we ought to get her to hospital," Whacker suggested. "That cut could need stitches."

"You can't tell till it's cleaned," May said. "Will you get a bowl and a clean cloth or tissues, Maura? And Imelda can put on the kettle."

"What d'you want me to do?" Mickser asked.

"You can get Patchie out of here!" May said, for he had slipped into the house with them and was happily casing the joint, snuffling around and doing his best to trip all of them up too.

"I'll do it," Richie said. "Here, Patchie!"

"I want you to run home and get me the elastoplast Mammy always keeps behind the clock," May said. "Take Patchie with you if you like. Will you bring over that other chair, Whacker? I want to put Mrs Reilly's feet up."

It was strange, Richie thought, as he ran off on his errand, how May had suddenly become the boss. Sometimes Whacker seemed to take command, if it was a question of technical know-how, but mostly everyone expected him to give the orders. Faced with somebody who was hurt for the second time in two days, both he and Whacker could think of nothing but getting help, yet May seemed to know exactly what to do. Maybe she ought to be a nurse. There wasn't much chance of her being a doctor. Where would they get the money for her to train for a job like that?

By the time May had gently sponged the cut with clean water it didn't look nearly so bad and the blood showed no signs of coming through the plaster. The colour began to return to Mrs Reilly's face as she sipped her tea, and she no longer looked so dazed.

"You won't tell your Mammy about this, sure you won't?" she asked May anxiously.

"Ah, no, Mrs Reilly," May promised. "We won't any of us say anything to anybody, will we?"

She looked around at the others and especially hard at Imelda, who always found the keeping of secrets difficult.

"Cross my heart and hope to die," Imelda said and the boys all nodded.

"Then," Mrs Reilly said, "I must go to work."

"Are you sure you're able, Mammy?" Maura asked anxiously.

"I am, of course," her mother insisted, "only I don't feel like facing Ma tonight. I'll go see her in the morning, first thing."

"It's none of my business," Whacker said, "but I'd he happier if the money was paid over tonight. Could Maura not take it for you?"

"I don't know would she be able for Ma," her mother said. "She'd want to be sure to get a receipt and Ma doesn't like putting anything down on paper."

"And there's my book to be got back too," Maura said. "I'd be afraid she wouldn't give it me."

"Whacker and me will go too, Mrs Reilly," Richie said. "We'll be well able for her and she'll not try anything on if there's others there to see her."

So after they had walked Mrs Reilly as far as the bus stop, Richie, Whacker and Maura climbed the stone steps to the third floor of Block B of the Flats and knocked on Ma Mulcahy's door. Ma herself opened the door to them. Without the familiar red coat and with an apron tied around her waist she looked different somehow. In fact, Maura thought, she simply looked like Jemmo and Patser's mother. She had been laying the table for the tea when they knocked and there was a pleasant smell of frying in the little flat.

"I'm Maura Reilly," Maura explained. "Mammy couldn't come herself, so she sent me down with the sixteen pound for the week."

"Fair enough," Ma said, holding out her hand for the money.

"Hang on a moment, Maura," Whacker cut in. "Let's get a receipt for it first."

"That's a quare way to do business," Ma said, though Maura thought there was a hint of laughter in her voice. "Receipts are for money given, not promised!"

"We can make an exchange," Richie said, "like they do with spies."

"Sounds like you don't trust me, lads," Ma said and this time she was definitely laughing, but she took a book from the mantlepiece, wrote in it and tore out a page.

"Now," she said, "let's see the colour of your money."

Maura took the notes from her pocket and gave them to Ma, taking the receipt in return.

"Does it say how much is still owing?" Whacker asked suspiciously.

Maura nodded, showing him the bit of paper with Ma's round, almost childish handwriting on it.

"That's what Mammy said was still owing," she told him.

"You see!" Ma said. "There'd be no problem at all if people would only keep up with their payments."

"Things have been hard at home," Maura explained, "but we'll be able to keep them up from this out."

"So there's no need for you to be holding the allowance book," Richie added.

"One swallow doesn't make a summer," Ma said. "Let's see how she does next week, before we make any change in our arrangements."

"We'll see nothing of the sort," Whacker said truculently, squaring his shoulders and trying to look as tough as Jemmo. "You've no right to hold that book anyways. You could be reported for the like of that!"

"And I could tell Mr Reilly how his wife borrowed money over the Christmas and still hasn't paid it back," Ma snapped. "And wouldn't it be the right thing for me to do? Isn't he the head of the household and wouldn't a bank be looking for his signature? Not that a bank would ever give a loan without security the way I do."

"So tell him!" Richie replied, but Maura interrupted him.

"Ah no, Mrs Mulcahy!" she cried. "Please don't say anything to me Da!"

Ma flashed a triumphant smile at Whacker.

"That's the way of it," she said, "and fair exchange is no robbery. You hold your tongue and I'll hold mine."

"It's no fair exchange when one party has more to tell," Whacker argued. "There are other things worth the telling. Things like the way people get slipped a few bob for giving evidence when other people fall into pot holes by mistake-on-purpose!"

The smile vanished from Ma Mulcahy's face, and her eyes became hard.

"You won't find many around here to shed tears over an informer," she said coldly. "Not even if he should chance to have some class of an accident."

"Whacker's no informer," Richie said doggedly. "He was only saying the exchange isn't fair if the score's not even!"

"And who says life is ever fair?" Ma wanted to know. "If the young wan wants her father kept in ignorance, there's a price to be paid. That's the way things are, like it or lump it."

"That's easy said when it isn't you has to be pinching and scraping," Maura cried, but Ma swung round to face her, her eyes blazing.

"You'll get no sympathy out of me," she shouted. "I've nothing only contempt for little snivellers full of self-pity. D'yous think you're the only ones ever had to face trouble? There are thousands like yous and crying about it gets them nowhere. D'yous think I was never in trouble? D'yous think I like having to go around banging on doors trying to get people to pay up what they owe? But what was I to do when my man died and left me with two small sons to rear? I knew his work as well as he did himself but the firm he worked for didn't want a woman calling door-to-door collecting their rents. So I looked for other work and when I couldn't get it, I took the bit of insurance money that was coming to me and went into the lending business. There's some say I charge over the odds, but it's a high-risk business, lending without security. If it wasn't, wouldn't the banks all be at it themselves?"

Maura stared at her in surprise.

"I'm sorry", she said. "I didn't know."

"And why would you?" Ma snapped. "I never went around whinging about life not being fair. I make sure I get paid what's owing to me, one way or another, and if it means being bad-mouthed by the likes of you I'll put up with it. You don't make a living at the lending business by being soft!"

"Then I'll tell you straight," Richie said. "We'll be making enough money in the next few weeks to pay off what Mrs Reilly owes, but we want that book gave back to her. The fuzz questioned us today over an accident, but we never said anything to them about the injury claims or the allowance book. What's more, we never said a thing about Jemmo and Patser being mixed up in it!"

The effect on Ma Mulcahy was remarkable. It was as if Richie had hit her across the face. For a second she looked totally defeated. Then she pulled herself together.

"Who said anything about Jemmo and Patser?" she blustered.

"No-one," Richie told her. "But a client of theirs was in a hit-and-run yesterday."

"That's no skin off of my nose. They're not responsible for what their friends do."

"I didn't say 'friends'," Richie cut in. "I said 'client'. They fixed up a car for him after the accident and the fuzz are sniffing around. They were looking for a description of the driver, but they didn't get it because I thought it would lead them to Jemmo and Patser."

"But yous will if I don't give back the book. Is that what you're saying?"

Richie shook his head.

"Jemmo and Patser go up to the ball alley," he said. "I couldn't tell on them. But I think they could be in trouble. It's not just the fuzz that's looking for them. There's Tiny Tim."

"Who?"

Richie told her then about the man with the sledgehammer fists and his determination to get his revenge.

"And, what's more," he concluded, "I don't blame him. Tony was hurted bad and he's a right to compensation. He didn't fall by accident-on-purpose like some I could name and he can't afford to be doing deals with 'witnesses'. If I was you, I'd tell Jemmo and Patser to get rid of that shed. It's too easy for whoever done a car job to hit someone on the way and next time they could kill them outright maybe."

Ma Mulcahy looked at him for a moment. Then she took Maura's allowance book out of her bag and handed it to her.

"Take it," she said, "and get out of here! And tell your Mammy to be sure and pay me the sixteen pound on time next week or I'll get it back off her, no matter what."

"And d'you know what," Maura told May when they got back, "I kinda felt sorry for her, till I remembered the way she'd tormented me Mammy."

"That's why Mrs Reilly has to join the Credit Union," May said. "Then she'll never need go near Ma any other time. Did she say she would?"

"I didn't get to ask her yet," Maura admitted.

"Oh, Maura! You promised!"

"I know, but she was upset over what happened. And then Richie and Whacker came with us to the bus stop. She'd never get talking about it with anyone else there. I'll talk to her in the morning."

"But you didn't give the extra one pound twenty to Ma against next week's money, did you?"

"Ah, no. I have it safe, but Mammy's sure to ask me for it in the morning. She'll want to buy something with it or give it to Mac to take something off of what's owing for groceries."

"But you mustn't let her!" May cried. "There'll be more money tomorrow she can have for the messages. This is special!"

"I don't see why," May argued. "Can't she use this for the messages and take a pound out of what we get tomorrow for the Credit Union?"

May shook her head obstinately.

"It has to be out of the first money we make," she said.

"But why?"

"Because Danny said, that's the why! Because if it's to be the second then maybe she'd leave it to the third or the fourth or the fifth and she'd keep putting it off and then maybe something would happen and that way she might never get around to it. Anyways, that's what Danny said and he made me promise I'd take them my very first pound."

"But Mammy never promised," Maura pointed out, "and I don't know will she do it. She needs the money real bad. Still, I'll talk to her."

And with that, May had to be content for the time being. Besides, she had other worries. As she dried the tea things that Richie had already washed, she wondered for the umpteenth time had she been crazy to tell Old Baldy Conscience so much about the Reillys. And then there was the photo. She had told Richie nothing at all about that. He had been too busy with the lighters and sunglasses at the time to ask what she had been doing in Bewley's. She had been afraid he would quiz her after he got home, but the encounter with Tiny Tim and all that followed seemed to have put the whole thing out of his mind. Now he had gone up to the ball alley with Whacker. She had been amazed at their going.

"Where d'you get the energy?" she had asked. "Won't we be on our feet all day at the selling tomorrow as well?"

Richie had only laughed at her.

"You talk like an ould one," he had said. "Won't we be long enough dead?"

"Sure, we're only going for a couple of games," Whacker had told her as they sauntered out, but now the light had gone from the sky and still they had not come back.

"Them two has gone off somewhere," she said to her mother. "It's too dark to be playing at this hour."

"Ah, well, it isn't as if they'd school in the morning," her mother replied. "They'll be back soon enough."

She might not have been so calm about it if she had known the trouble they were in.

They had finished their game when the light started to go. Whacker had beaten Richie as usual but, after the success of their mission to Ma Mulcahy, they were both in high spirits as they set out for home.

"Two weeks should be enough to put an end to the street trading," Whacker said. "We should easily have raised enough to pay off what's owing by then, unless we get a lot more rain."

"I won't be sorry either," Richie replied. "I can think of better ways to spend the holidays."

"I dunno," Whacker argued. "I think it's gas. I wouldn't mind carrying on on my own account if Tony's still in hospital. I know Mickser wants to."

"Maybe it's better on O'Connell Bridge and in Henry Street," Richie said. "You or Mickser can try doing the bank tomorrow."

"There's no need for anyone to do it," Whacker pointed out. "Two can work Henry Street, one with lighters and one with sunglasses."

They were passing the end of the lane and Richie noticed that the door to the shed was open.

"Jemmo and Patser must be expecting a client," he began, but he got no further.

From the darkness of a doorway opposite two figures suddenly emerged without warning. Taking the boys completely by surprise in a running tackle, they knocked them sideways through the open door of the shed. Richie heard the door slam shut behind them just before he hit the concrete floor.

9
BLACK OUT

ursing his bruised shoulder, Richie raised his head from the ground to see Jemmo Mulcahy looming over him. He twisted sharply away as Jemmo lashed out at him so his boot made forcible contact with the base of Richie's spine. As he contorted with pain, he heard Whacker yelp. Patser was doing a job on him too.

"That's what you get for informing on us!" he heard Jemmo shout.

"I didn't inform on anyone!" he yelled, before another spasm of pain struck him.

"Liar!" Jemmo cried. "Didn't Patser see you?"

Again the boot caught him, this time in the ribs. He tried to wriggle away, but found himself pinned against the shed wall. They were going to be pulverized!

Suddenly the shed door burst open. Engulfed in pain, Richie lay still, conscious only that the blows had ceased. He felt air on his face. Then he heard a woman's voice.

"Stop that before I murder the pair of yous! Yous needn't think yous are too big for me to take your father's belt to yous!"

Wincing, Richie struggled to get to his feet but the pain in his back and side made him give up. He fell back against the wall in a half-sitting position. Now he could see Jemmo and Patser, facing their mother like two small children caught stealing jam.

"They informed agin us, Ma!" Jemmo protested.

"An ass would have more sense that what yous have." Ma Mulcahy looked at her two sons with contempt. "If that pair had squealed to the rozzers yous would have been picked up long ago. And do yous think yous would get off the lighter for having murdered the pair of them? Yous make me sick! And I came to tell yous I want the pair of yous and all your gear out of here before morning. I have the place sold."

"Ah, Ma!" Jemmo began, but Ma Mulcahy cut in on him.

"And yous needn't be ah–Ma–ing me! I'd a right to sell it long ago, soon as I found out it wasn't wanted for the office development. I bought it cheap off of the fruit company when the markets closed down because I thought I'd get ten times the price from the developers. Now I want yous out of it so yous better get started on the packing. And I hope for your sake them two aren't bad hurted."

She came over to Richie then.

"Can you stand?" she asked.

Richie nodded. He didn't quite trust his voice and he wasn't going to disgrace himself in front of Ma Mulcahy. She helped him to his feet and ran an expert hand over his spine and rib cage.

"Did a right job on you, didn't they?" she commented, as Richie winced at her touch. "But I don't think they broke any bones. If the pain doesn't ease in a day or so, you'd better go looking for an X-ray, but I'd say you'll be better before you're twice married. A wiry little fella like you ought to be able for a bit of bruising without running to the doc. How about your pal?"

Whacker had got to his feet unaided. His face was cut and he had a swelling around his right eye. He gave them a rather twisted grin.

"When I said Tiny Tim would be worse, I didn't reckon on them jumping us from behind," he grunted.

"Cowardly sods," Ma said, "and you half their size, but don't worry. They'll be the sorry lads when I'm finished with them. Jemmo thinks because he's fifteen and a great lump of a lad that he's Mister Big, but he's no match for me. D'yous want me to help yous home?"

Richie shook his head again. It was bad enough to be going home with all the signs of a beating without the added humiliation of being helped by a woman, however tough. All the same, there was comfort in the sight of Jemmo, looking like a whipped cur as he began loading cans of spray paint into a crate. Car thieves were going to have to find somewhere else to get their cars resprayed and someone else to do the job for them.

By next morning, the whole right side of Richie's body was black and purple. Every movement was painful and he had to leave the selling to the others for, as Whacker remarked, he was "in no state to be playing hide-and-go-seek with the fuzz and he hobbling like he had the arthritis worse than old Danny."

"Howanever," Whacker continued, "your bruises are worth framing. There's no way Ma Mulcahy will come looking for the return of Maura's allowance book so long as you're hanging around like a turkey left over from Christmas on a fishmonger's hook!"

So it was that Richie was sitting on a chair in the sun outside the Byrnes' door reading a comic, for all the world like old Danny with one of his library books, when Bridie Taylor called. Richie had never spoken to her before but he knew at once who she was. Mrs Doyle had sent one of the young ones out of the flats up to the presbytery to see her when she was at her wits' end over a sick child needing special food and nothing only the unmarried mother's allowance to buy it out of. Bridie Taylor was the Vincent de Paul woman.

"Is your mother in?" she asked Richie.

"She went for the messages," he told her, wondering why the Vincent de Paul woman would be calling on his mother.

"Isn't that your sister?" she asked, holding out a copy of a newspaper with a photo which took up nearly half the top of the page.

Richie reached out for the paper and winced with pain. Then he winced a second time at what he saw. It was an excellent photo and there was no mistaking May, offering her tray of sunglasses to the bus queue, eagerness and anxiety mingling in her expression. He would like to have said it was no-one he knew, but what was the use? Anyone in the Square would tell her the truth. He nodded stiffly.

"Father Tom was sure it was. Is she at home?"

Richie shook his head. How could May have been foolish enough to let anyone take a snap like that? They would be in right trouble now. And then this one had to come around busybodying. If she had kept out of it maybe no-one in the Square would know anything about it. The paper wasn't one they ever bought. He wondered was it worth trying to get the Vincent de Paul woman to keep her mouth shut. He studied her face. It was a nice face and she looked him straight in the eye when she spoke. He decided to give it a go.

"D'you have to show that to Ma?" he asked. "She's going to be awful upset. She doesn't know May was out selling?"

The woman looked at him thoughtfully.

"It depends if I can find out what I need to know without talking to her," she said. "Maybe you can help me?"

"What d'you want to know?"

"Your sister told the reporter about a friend's mother, who was in trouble with a moneylender," she said. "I could help that woman if I could only find her."

"She's getting help already," Richie said abruptly. He knew Mrs Reilly would die at the thought of her story being on the paper and all the world knowing about it.

"From your sister and her friends," Bridie Taylor said. "But there's a better way than having them break the law, even if they're doing it to help someone and not doing much harm when all's said and done."

Richie was getting fed up with being made suffer for keeping other people's secrets. Besides, with May's photo in her hand she would get the information soon enough anyway.

"If I tell you who May was talking about," he asked, "will you have to tell her that it's on the paper?"

"You can leave that to me," Bridie Taylor said. "And you can be sure I'll say nothing in front of her husband. I'm here to try to help, not add to anyone's troubles."

Richie decided she was to be trusted. He directed her to Reillys' house and watched her cross the Square and knock on the door. She was a friendly sort of person, he thought, and when you got talking to her she didn't seem much older than Liz Meany from next door, who had gone to England to look for work.

Mrs Reilly herself opened the door. Watching from behind his comic, the way he had seen plainclothesmen on the telly watching suspects from behind their newspapers, Richie noticed she was wearing her head-scarf as if she were about to go out, but she exchanged a few words with Bridie and then let her in to the house and closed the door behind them. Some twenty minutes later, he saw the two of them come out of the house, cross the square and disappear around the corner in the direction of Greek Street.

When his mother came back from Mac's he said nothing to her about Bridie Taylor and the newspaper. But then he had said nothing to her the previous evening about what had happened to Whacker and himself. There was no way he could have hidden the fact that he had been hurt, of course, but that was easily explained.

"I fell real hard up at the ball alley," he told her. "I thought I'd busted my side it's that sore!"

His mother accepted the explanation easily enough. She was well used to her sons coming home with cuts and bruises, but May had looked at him questioningly and later on he had told her the whole story. He had been more honest with her than she had been with him, he thought now. The more he thought about her having told their secret plans to a newspaper reporter the angrier he got. And she hadn't said a word to anyone! By the time the girls got back he had worked himself into a fury.

"Mickser's gone to Loftus Lane with Whacker," May explained by way of greeting. "He's letting on to have taken your place for the day, but we got World Cup caps and scarves today and they sold great. We got eighty-two quid even though you weren't there!"

"Nothing to what we'll get from Da when he sees today's paper," Richie snapped. "And if I wasn't near-crippled I'd beat you myself for spilling the beans to that reporter. It's the very last time I'll ever tell you anything I don't want broadcast to the world!"

May went white.

"But he promised it wouldn't be on the paper for weeks!" she cried.

"So he broke his promise," Richie retorted, "the very same as you broke yours when you talked to him after promising not to tell! And how well you said nothing about it to any of the rest of us!"

"She told me!" Maura declared loyally, but Richie rounded on her, sending pain tearing at his side in the process.

"Then you'd a right to warn the rest of us!" he shouted, the pain only increasing his anger. "Aren't we all in this together? Girls! Yous all make me sick!"

"You needn't be including me!" Imelda declared, tossing her head. "I knew nothing whatsoever about it. And if yous want to fight about it yous can do it without me!"

She ran off across the Square to her own house and, after a moment of awkwardness, Maura followed her.

Tea was an unusually silent meal at the Byrne's that evening, with only Brendan's childish chatter and the baby's shouts to interrupt their thoughts, while Mr Byrne studied the sports pages of the evening paper, and May glanced uneasily at her mother.

"Yous are very quiet," her mother said finally. "If your side's that bad, Richie, maybe you'd better go over to the hospital and get it seen to."

"It's all right, Ma. Don't be making a fuss!" Richie grunted ungraciously.

May pushed her chair back from the table. She hadn't even finished her sausages and mash. Coming home she had felt hungry enough, but her appetite had vanished since the row with Richie. The trouble was that she had no defence against his accusations. Everything he had said was true. She must have been mad to have trusted old Baldy Conscience.

"I'm going out for a while, Ma," she said, "but you can leave the things. I'll do them later."

Without even waiting for a reply, she ran out into the Square. Once the door had closed behind her, she hesitated. She was tired from the day's selling and had no wish to go anywhere, but she had had to get out of the house. Richie was black out with her and her parents would be too if only they knew. How long would it be before someone ran in to tell them? She could picture Mrs Doyle, all excited at having a piece of gossip to share, thrusting the paper under her mother's nose.

"Isn't it a great likeness altogether?" she would cry. "And do you mean to say May never told you a thing about it? Isn't she the secretive one?"

May thought of going across to Imelda. She needed to talk to someone and Imelda was supposed to be her best friend, but Whacker would be there and of course he'd side with Richie. Worse still, Imelda might be black out with her too. She had obviously been angry to find that May had told Maura all about it without telling her.

May decided to talk to Maura instead. More and more often in the last year she had found herself wanting to talk to Maura rather than Imelda. She supposed Imelda had noticed that too. That was probably why she was so huffy all the time, but May couldn't help secretly thinking now of Maura as more than just her second-best friend.

She tapped on the door of Maura's house and waited. She hoped there wasn't a row going on there. Maura's father was home. She had seen him crossing the Square just before her mother had called her to come in to her tea.

Maura opened the door herself and May could hardly recognize her. Her pale, freckled face was alight and her green eyes glowed with happiness.

"Oh, May," she whispered, pulling May away from the house and closing the door behind her, "I was just coming over to you to tell you: everything's turned out great!"

May looked at her in amazement. She herself had been feeling so low that she had gone to Maura looking for a shoulder to weep on. Now here was Maura, whom she spent so much time trying to comfort, apparently on top of the world.

"Did your father get a job then?" she asked.

Maura shook her head.

"No," she answered, "but he told Mammy he was sorry, in front of me and everything!"

"How come?" May asked her.

"It's all because of you really," Maura said breathlessly, "on account of the Vincent de Paul woman seeing the piece on the paper. She called over to see Mammy and she was real nice and friendly and understood everything like. And it was real lucky she came when she did on account of me Mammy was just going to Mac's with the one pound twenty she got off of me."

"You couldn't get her to take it to the Credit Union then?" May asked, disappointed. Maura's great news didn't sound that great at all, she thought.

"No, but the Vincent de Paul woman did. And she went with her and talked to the lady there. And now Manny's a member and she's going to give them a bit of money every week instead of giving it to Ma Mulcahy."

"But what about Ma? Won't she give out and come looking for your book back if she doesn't get her money?"

"She's paid off," Maura replied. "The Credit Union lent Mammy the money to pay her and the Vincent de Paul woman went with her and they done it right away."

"That's great!" May said. "So she didn't need the money we got for today's selling at all!"

"Oh yes, she did," Maura cried. "That's the best part of it. The Credit Union people gave her a bit extra, because the woman said she needed it for the housekeeping and with that and the money we got today she went down to Leventon's and got her coat and ring out of the pawn. When she showed the ring to me Da, she said she'd found it in the lining of the coat; that it must have slipped through a hole in the pocket like. That's when Da told her he was sorry for the things he'd said and now they're talking like they used when I was little, so I want to leave them on their own till me Mammy has to go to work."

"Pity she has to go," May said.

She was glad things were so good at the Reillys'. All the same, she didn't share

Maura's certainty that it would last. Wouldn't Mr Reilly be his old self again as soon as he had next week's allowance in his pocket and the price of an evening in Flynn's? But nothing could dampen Maura's optimism.

"Maybe she won't have to do the cleaning much longer," she said. "Me Da may be getting work."

"Has he word of a job then?" May asked.

"No," Maura said, "but he was saying he was going to try calling round the houses the way we did on the North Circular that time. To see if anyone wants any windows cleaned or grass cut or cars washed or sheds painted or anything.

May tried to hide her surprise. Mr Reilly must be a changed man indeed.

"He says there's plenty of money to be picked up like that if you could put your pride in your pocket," Maura continued. "And when Michael Casey gets back from his holidays maybe he could find me something in RTE for a week or two anyways. And if he doesn't, there's always the selling. I mean, I'm getting quite good at it now and Whacker and Mickser want to go on with it even if you and Richie and Imelda don't."

May wondered how it would all work out. She had heard her father say a dozen times that a working man should have the dignity of a proper job and not be doing nixers on the Labour. But then the same should be true for the working woman and there wasn't much dignity about part-time work at the contract cleaning. It was certainly a change for the better that Mr Reilly was willing to do his share and even if his change of heart didn't last, didn't Maura deserve to be happy so long as it did? She would keep her fears to herself.

Suddenly May realized that Maura had given her something much better than a shoulder to cry on. She had made what May had done seem good! What did it matter if Richie was black out with her? It was talking to old Baldy Conscience that had brought the Vincent de Paul woman to call on Mrs Reilly and it was that that had made Maura happy.

May started to laugh. She took Maura's two hands and swung her around and around like they used to do when they were both little. She didn't stop swinging until they were both out of breath and collapsed on to the edge of the concrete near the children's slide in the middle of the Square. Then she remembered old Danny.

He had been right about the Credit Union. She would definitely keep her promise about giving them a pound out of her first week's wages. But now she had some advice for Danny.

"If you're ever in real trouble, Danny," she would say to him, "go and see the Vincent de Paul woman. Because she's not a stuck-up do-gooder at all. She really does help people."

Robbers on TV
by
Carolyn Swift

Maura, Whacker and May find intrigue
in the television studios and behind the
scenes.

Children's
POOLBEG

*Irish Myths and Tales for
Young People*
by
Carolyn Swift

This new collection contains fourteen ancient
Irish tales, told so that young readers can enjoy
all their heroism and treachery, magic and
romance, fun and foolishness. There are tales of
daring athletes and boastful champions, beauti-
ful girls changed into butterflies or fawns, wise
women who outwit armies, murderous kings,
wicked step-mothers, one-eyed giants, sinister
druids and mysterious sea voyages. All play
their part in this enthralling kaleidoscope of
Irish legends.

Children's
POOLBEG

A Likely Story
by
Mary Lavin

Packy is the only son of a poor widow and they
live in a tumbledown cottage in Ireland. He has
heard whispers of Little People and gold hoards
and changelings. His mother dismisses these
tales as "likely stories" but Packy is not so sure.
For some time he thinks he has seen out of the
corner of his eye a beckoning hand. Then, one
day, on his way home from school he meets a
mysterious little man...

This is a story, likely or not, that will keep you
reading to the end.

Children's
POOLBEG

The Long March
by
Michael Mullen

After the battle of Kinsale, on the last day of the year 1602, O'Sullivan Beare left Glengarriff in County Cork with one thousand followers, the remnants of a race defeated by the English in a cruel war. They set out to reach the safety of O'Rourke's castle in Leitrim. Two weeks later only thirty-five people reached their goal. The rest had perished on the way or abandoned the march.

Michael Mullen recreates one of the most remarkable episodes in Irish history in this gripping and stirring novel for young readers.

Children's
POOLBEG